B O Y

There is a Tide
The Rape of Sita
Getting Rid of It
Mutiny

BOY

Lindsey Collen

BLOOMSBURY

First published in Great Britain in 2004

Copyright © 2004 by Lindsey Collen

The moral right of the author has been asserted

Bloomsbury Publishing Plc, 38 Soho Square, London W1D 3HB

The translated and adapted excerpt from 'Ti-Bato Papye'
by Alain Fanchon on page 86 is taken from the anthology
Ti-Bato Papye published by Ledikasyon pu Travayer, Mauritius, 1989

A CIP catalogue record for this book
is available from the British Library

ISBN 0 7475 6387 X

10 9 8 7 6 5 4 3 2 1

Typeset by Hewer Text Ltd, Edinburgh
Printed in Great Britain by Clays Ltd, St Ives plc

All papers used by Bloomsbury Publishing are natural,
recyclable products made from wood grown in
well-managed forests. The manufacturing processes conform
to the environmental regulations of the country of origin.

At home they call me 'Boy'. Both of them. I'm telling you.

Enough to make you puke.

Not that I ever *said* anything about it to them. What's the point?

Anyway, I'm not going to make you sit and read about scenery or anything like that. And I'm not going to preach morals at anyone either.

I'm just going to tell what happened that day, the day results came out. The day she sent me off like that. The truth. That kind of thing.

But let me give you the picture first.

Of at my folks' place.

It's like she calls me 'Boy', my mother does, and like in the next breath, she says, 'Look!' And there she stands, pointing up at the photograph of her father-in-law, who is my granddad, hanging up on the hallway wall. Her gold and silver bracelets clatter down from her wrist when she lifts her arm up like that. I can hear them now, I tell you. The fancy green and pink pattern of her silk shawl as she pulls it over her arm, a kind of screen that bars my view. And then there's her eau-de-toilette. It flies out into that whole dark hallway, like it hits my nostrils.

You get the idea? An invading army.

When she isn't making a racket with her bangles, our

house is a silent place. Too quiet, if you ask me. Sickly quiet. Deadly quiet. I don't know why it's like that.

So, anyway, as usual I *obey*. That's the problem with me. I listen too much.

I look up at my granddad's photo. Why? Because she told me to. But this time, I actually see it. The first thing I see is the heavy wooden frame. No joke. Like the frame is more important than the photo. And they've hung the thing far too high up, for a start. Everything about it gets me. He stands there, my granddad, Mr Self-Importance himself. Mr Certainty. Mr Conviction. In his cream and gold wedding toque. Eyeing the camera like he thinks he's a film star. His bride, that's my granny, has got her head covered in red and gold satin, her forehead bowed down with the jewellery, her eyes lowered. But maybe she's not so bad, I don't know. Maybe she feels them all making her do that stupid cowering like that. Maybe I discern a filament of burning resentment in her attitude. Maybe. Just under her skin in the photo. Maybe. Just under those eyelids of hers.

Maybe she's on my side.

But I doubt it. Nobody is.

All this is just to give you an idea of our house, you know, without boring you with the gaudy curtains or anything like that.

'Look at him, Boy!' she yells, I tell you. She makes me jump sometimes. In all that silence. 'Already married when he was your age.'

Stale news.

'*And*,' she adds, '*and* he was already planting potatoes. Planting potatoes *interline*. At your age, Boy!'

Fucking hell.

See, she calls me 'Boy' again. In the same sentence.

2

I could kill her.

Anyway, like I said, it's a bad day. It's fetching-exam-results day.

So there I am, standing eating my cornflakes by the kitchen sink. My mother is sweeping around my feet with a *balye fatak*, her other hand behind her back. Like I'm a lamp stand. We don't eat breakfast together any more, the three of us. So she says: 'Go on! Wash your hands now, Boy. Pull yourself together a bit. Go get into your father's car now.'

If you ask me, she can't actually *see* me. She looks right past.

Or right through.

'I'm *eating*, Ma,' I say, pointedly.

'I know,' she says. You see she knows everything about me. No need for me to say anything. She already knows it.

So I put down my cornflakes, just like that, in the sink.

Teach her, I think. Not that I'm not sure anyone could *teach* her anything.

You know what she does last night? Just to give you an idea.

You wouldn't believe it.

Pisses me off just remembering it. I'm ashamed, really, when I think of it. Of *myself*. But here it is. It's the truth.

She comes up to me, sits right next to me on the edge of the armchair I'm in. I'm watching some dumb television programme and eating supper at the same time. Yes, she sits there and puts her hand across into my plate, my own plate, on my own knee in front of me, and she takes a bit of my rice, some fish curry, and then some chutney, moulds it all nicely into a chewable ball, and pops her fingers into my mouth, and flicks the food off on to my tongue with her thumb. She feeds me. What d'you think of that?

And I let her. That's what bugs me.

It's a wonder she doesn't come up to me in the toilet and wash my arse after I've finished crapping.

It's a wonder I don't let her. Talk about a fucking mummy's little boy.

Usually I never swear.

Usually, I do everything she says. That's my problem. Like I said. Usually I would just wash my hands like she says. I would just go out to my father's car like she says.

Only, not today.

Oh no.

Instead, I just put my cornflakes down and storm out, back into my room instead. And I slam the door behind me for good measure.

I shock myself today.

I hear her mumble 'histrionics'.

I just stand there in the middle of my room.

Lonely. As a fucking cloud.

Then, with my right hand, I pick up the blade from behind my geometry set on my desk, and I pick up a sheet of a mock exam paper with my left hand and hold it up against the morning light. I dig the blade into the middle of the top edge of the sheet of paper, and try to cut downwards. A sudden diagonal slit splits the paper in two. One half ends up dangling downwards from a sliver of paper holding it to the other half. Looking ridiculous. That's what I feel like. That bottom bit of paper, dangling. Gives me the creeps.

I shove the blade quick back behind the geometry set. The 'Krish Burton' etched on the lid of the metal box is crossed out. That's me. Crossed out.

I imagine myself sitting naked at my desk. Stunted. Skinny. Naked.

Ridiculous.

Came into the world naked, they say, so I can go out again naked. They mean 'money' when they say that.

'And so *dark* for a baby,' I overheard my mother saying this about me the other day, 'And slimy.'

'A breech,' she added. Not that I know what that means, come to think of it. Womentalk. Probably means I came out in breach of good manners. 'He was *much* worse than the first.' That's what she says. *Much worse than the first.*

Naked I see myself, as I open the desk drawer in front of me. Inside I find a snake of turquoise-coloured rope.

On the window sill, there is a tiny seethrough plastic bag with stuff in it that's a bit *too* white. Next to it stands this bright orange plastic one-litre bottle of Fanta, the rising sun just beginning to shine through it. That's what most of them do. Like it's the colour that gets them. Backdrop of a pure blue sky. Or a turquoise lagoon.

Talking about colours, under my bed I've got this old Raja Oil bottle full of pale pink liquid. And a box of Joker matches. It's got this picture of a joker from a pack of cards on it.

Talk about keeping my options open.

'Boy!'

It's *his* voice now. It's coming from out there. Alien space. Our house is like that. It echoes empty. You'd think we didn't have any furniture. But the place is full of it. Like a furniture shop. But still, to me it echoes empty.

'Boy!'

Don't you ever call me that again!

I don't actually say that. I never tell them. I don't even answer him.

Play dead, I do, instead.

5

I mull over the word 'histrionics'. I could wipe out my impotence with any one of those acts.

'Boy, let's go get your results now, Boy! Come along now! Boy!' He is a quiet man, my father. Plodding his weary way. That's how I see him. Always present and always absent. At the same time. You ever heard of such a thing?

Present and absent?

If only.

If only I could just not be here at all. If only I could be somewhere else.

'Boy!'

I've been counting, I don't know about you. That makes it six times he's called me 'Boy' since I got back to my room. Six times. Beat that.

I sit and stare into the longan tree by my window. Not a single longan this year. Not one. If only I could just stretch my arm out through the burglar guards and pick one. Baya said it's like as you bite into the hard shell-skin, there's this wild sweet taste when the fruit's flesh bursts out, squirting perfume up the inside of your nose. It could make a person drunk with pleasure. That's what he said. It could transport a person to another place, he said. It's like an orgasm, he said.

If only.

Or.

If only.

Or, if only I could *be* a something else instead of being me. Maybe a something huge and seethrough, something moving outwards, blowing up, distending, spreading out thinner and thinner like a bubble, out into the sky, then getting so thin that it turns into ether and it's gone. That kind of something.

'Boy!'

Seven.

Or, if only I could like, shrink, and then go on shrinking, and then, when I'm small enough, slide down into some crevice that would open up in front of me on the surface of the earth, starting to appear on the polished bright red-cement floor of my room, here. I could just slip in. And then the earth, having swallowed me, could close up again. Leaving nothing but a hairline crack. Observed only by the most observant of researchers studying the mystery of my disappearance. Ha! Ha! As if anyone would miss me. Maybe they would wonder at the mark. Maybe my mother would just fill it up with red Brito wax, and polish it with her foot on a half-coconut brush.

I'm in a bad way. As you can see. Full of self-pity.

'Bo-oy!'

It's in two syllables now, *Bo-oy*.

I don't move. Maybe he'll go away. But, of course, I know he won't.

No such luck.

Instead, my mother chimes in, too. 'Boy!' she shrieks. The word rasps in my ears as if it were full of consonants or even sibilants. And I hear those bangles of hers tilt into one another, signalling she has lifted her arms up in despair.

A mynah up the longan tree walks along the branch by my window and then stops against that empty blue sky, looks at me with intense hatred from out of its one black eye in its golden-yellow eye paint. Then it copies them, squawking: 'Boy!'

'Shut your fucking mouth!' I reply to the bird.

*

But I'm worried. What if this name they call me makes me grow up stunted? I am already quite stunted enough for my age, thank you.

My father jingles his car keys in his pocket.

Now that is one sound I can't stand.

'Boy!' My father again.

I turn around and look at the door. Closed. Cream paint peeling off it. It was grey before, you can see.

Then I see the Boy George poster. Pastels. It used to belong to *him*. To Baya.

Boy George. *Boy*. He's also called *Boy*. Funny, I never realized that before.

'Boy!' Both voices at once now. A duet. I still don't answer. I don't move a muscle. I know they won't actually form a posse and come and pull me out of my room. Not prise me out unwillingly, a snail from its shell. Not today, anyway.

One day last week, she just breezed in, singing some Lata Mangeskar number from an old Indian film from her lost youth.

Lost.

The word *lost* frightens me. Even if I *think* it.

Anyway, like a missile, she came in. Camouflaged in shocking pinks and grasshopper greens. Breezing in to check on my school uniform.

On her little baby Boy's uniform. As if she hadn't even held the service for shaving off my *seve bondye* yet.

Blade cuts rope. Rope ties up powder. Powder covers blade.

Joker burns all.

✳

8

'Boy, what's keeping you?' It's *her* again, only in her voice I can hear a shrill note of consternation. She knows I'm nervous. Senses it. She knows everything about me. She knows I'm scared shitless of results.

The other day she took me to the doctor's.

You won't believe this. But I said I'd tell you the truth. So here it is.

A woman doctor, it was. 'Where does it hurt?' You won't believe it, but *she* answers before I can. 'Here. Just here, doctor.' The doctor, I tell you, looks up at the ceiling. She prepares another question: 'When does it hurt, or hurt more?' Again, my mother knows: 'All the time. It's sore all the time, doctor,' she says.

The lady doctor starts to get pissed off, I can tell. My mother's not letting her do her job properly, so she says: 'Could you let him speak for himself, please, Mrs Burton?' But my mother can't. She can't help it. She goes on and on. Until the doctor has to say: 'Do me a favour, will you? Wait on the verandah for just a few moments. I'll have the nurse call you if need be. Go on then.' Just like that. So, it's not just me imagining things.

Another thing. She fishes around in my school things. Behind my back. Looking for cigarette stompies? I don't know. Or for bits of old newspaper that've been folded around some *chi chi* food from the bazaar? Or a single long hair from some girl's head?

If only.

'Boy, let's go. Let's get it over and done with.'

In his taxi, he means. Let *us* go and get *my* results in *his* taxi.

I can't find enough air to breathe in this place.

So, suddenly, I storm out of my room.

As usual, capitulation.

Abject capitulation.

My father is standing there. His shoulders droop, sort of. He is in his clean, open-necked shirt, nicely ironed, nicely buttoned up, and tucked neatly into his trousers, also nicely ironed with a crease down each leg. I panic. What if I grow up like him?

My mother comes hurry-scurrying after me, flurrying colours, catching me up on the verandah, and grabbing my head and pulling it down to her head, and kissing me goodbye. I wipe my cheek with the back of my hand.

'You left your cornflakes. You haven't even had your tea, Boy.' She's got this line in resentment, 'And don't you be cross, now!'

I open the back door of his shiny red taxi and get in. Government is threatening to outlaw old taxis like his. I'm fetched and I'm carried in it. I'm taken out and brought back in it. When I come out of a building, of any door or any gate, as soon as I look up, and who doesn't look up on coming out of a building, there the taxi is, standing right there in front of me, lying in wait for me, with the door already wide open.

To catch me.

I hate cars.

I hate this taxi.

When we go out as a family, my father and mother and I, some family, it's *naturally* my father who drives. Well, someone has to. My mother can't. She wouldn't even want to. I'm only seventeen so I can't even if I did want to. So he drives. Then it all starts. He breaks his silence. 'Should we stop and have something to eat?' He is kind. He is polite. But, he is in charge of when we eat and where. Bottom line, he decides. And when the food part is over, it's when and where to pee. He decides on that too.

Now, I am sitting in the back of the car as if my father is only my driver.

And off he drives. There are two kinds of taxi driver. One that drives too fast and one that drives too slow. My father is the kind that drives too slow.

Gradually, out of the window, I start seeing clumps of other boys under leafy-roofed skies. Gravitating, like me, to different bulletin boards full of exam results. All over the fucking country. So, why am I so different? From Karo Lalyann to Sen Zorz Road in Porlwi, I watch them. They are in groups for a start. Loud-talking bunches. They are walking, walking, walking. Meanwhile, I am sitting, sitting, sitting, closed in behind glassed-in windows, floating past them in the car. My dad, as always, sitting bolt upright behind the steering wheel, his dark glasses now wrapped around his face. He only brings them out once the passenger is firmly behind him. Can put a passenger off, he says.

He is proud of me. College boy. HSC exams. He thinks I go to a good school, Bhujoharry Medco. He thinks I'll do well in the exams.

As we get nearer, I begin to see my own classmates, from Bhujoharry Medco. There's a big magnet pulling at us all. Iron filings. Towards the dreaded bulletin board.

But for me it's not like for them. *They* catch buses, they ride bicycles, they walk. They've got choices. Which street to go down. Where to stop. What speed to go at. One well-built athletic boy called Jean-Pierre suddenly runs and takes a flying leap really high and grabs a late mango from a tree leaning over on to the pavement. Just because he wants to. We pass three boys who used to sit in the back of the class. They slouch over the handrail of the canal bridge, looking down at only they themselves know what beneath it. Another group is disappearing into a neon-lit shopping arcade. In broad daylight. Into the cyber café. A detour. Look at Devesh, walking with his hand almost holding the hand of that girl who is walking next to him. They accidentally keep touching one another. I watch their hands. Makes me feel excited. Stupid, isn't it?

But what can you expect from someone closed up in a car?

Four boys from the art class do a quick rap dance in the street. Look at them. My father has to step on his brake. Now they saunter, yes they *saunter*, into the tobacconist's. One lone boy, Zeel, leans against the wall of an advertising agency, and watches girl students passing by. Another one eats pickled green mango at a mango and cucumber seller's tricycle. *Imagine eating a bit of pickled cucumber with salt and chilli just because you want to.*

As for me, I can only watch them through the car window. Through glass. Through glass darkly.

My mother says they probably eat sausages.

She says you never know what they've put in them. Could get *mad cow disease*, she says. Pork in them, she says. 'Chi! Chi!' You never know, she says, insinuating it's dog meat or cat meat in them. Or eel or snake meat. Or the flesh of newborn monkeys. Or of dead hedgehogs. Or worse still, *beef*.

One boy pulls the cap off a friend's head and puts it back-to-front on his own.

Friend.

That's another word that gets me. It *affects* me. *Friend*. My chest tightens. My throat constricts.

I lean back on the car seat, sweat gluing my shirt to it, trying to escape from the effect of that one syllable.

For seven years, not a word of a lie, every single

morning, my father has brought me to the college gates in his taxi. Patiently, he has done this. He has never complained once. I hardly missed a day's school either. Always the same trip.

And every single afternoon, as I came out of the same school gate, there was his taxi, bright red, sitting waiting for me. Loyally.

I feel for a shirt button to undo. There's not enough air in here.

For my private tuition, for the past two years, it's the same story. He picks me up after school and drops me right at the teacher's garage gates in Zakob Road, and when I come out again, there he is. Waiting to take me straight home.

'Boy, I hope everything goes fine,' as he pulls up nervously in front of the Bhujoharry gates.

Quietly, so that he can't hear me, I distinctly say: 'Shut up, for fuck's sake!'

It must be my nerves. Like I said, I never swear.

Once in primary school I said '*Enn duk, sa,*' and the others all laughed at me, and started to point at me and to dance round me and chant, '*Enn duk, sa! Duk, sa!*'

Today swearwords line up in my larynx, just behind my tonsils.

'Yes, Dad,' I reply, swallowing them back.

I get out of his red taxi, and slam the door. I don't usually do that. I know it drives him mad. Not that he would *say* anything.

My arms don't swing. And they feel too long. *Ape-boy.*

Two or three boys skip past in the same direction as me, that means to *fetch* their results. They *skip*, I tell you. One of them has grown his hair long into a *churki* down his back, and another one has shaved all of his right off. They look *cool*.

One boy comes back in the opposite direction, and passes close by, almost touching my right hand. He is smiling a satisfied smile.

At the very same time, another boy is setting off home, his jaw set firmly, the corners of his mouth turned down, biting back tears, passing me on my left side.

Theatre masks. The comedy and the tragedy.

Fucking hell. It's like there's this great big winnowing basket. God is this old woman so fussy about sorting her rice, tossing us all into the air, again and again. The weak ones, the chaff, taken off by the wind, weeping, thrown away. The strong ones, heavy enough, good grain, kept, weighed and looked after. Useful. God knows what for, but useful.

I feel the eyes of the other boys on me as I get nearer. I read what they tell me.

'Shit.'

She's going to throw me away.

But I force my legs to go on walking, so that I can go and look with my own two eyes, see for myself, although I already know.

I look for my name. Look up and look down.

There it is. Burton, Krishnadev.

Fail.

'Bad luck, Krish,' a boy just behind me mumbles, confirming. I can't see who it is.

At school they call me 'Krish'.

Not that many of them speak to me.

Small mercies.

Everything's in black and white now.

I will not repeat. No repeaters' class for me. I will not do another year.

When I get back to the taxi: 'Boy,' my dad says, 'Boy, are your results bad?'

'Fail,' I tell him. 'Failed.'

'Never mind. That's life. Jayde, Boy. Next year. You can take the exams all over again. It doesn't matter, Boy. *You've* got two chances at the exam, Boy, you do.' He touches me lightly on my shoulder. But, of course, in his voice, you can't miss the disappointment. And not just that. Baya would have had only one chance to sit the exam. They count it from the month you're born in. And he would have passed. Brilliantly.

When he starts up the engine, he says: 'I'm leaving the car at Goolam Panelbeaters. Do you mind, Boy? Perhaps we could walk home from there? Car fitness test coming up.'

For once it's what I want to do.

He drives to Goolam Panelbeaters in Lakavern. There's like a whole flock of cars there, all colours, matchbox toys, nestling together in the thick shade of giant trees, all taken apart, each one in a different stage of being put together by Goolam Panelbeaters. And the smell of Duco spraypaint.

'He'll knock the car into shape for the government test next month,' my dad says. For taxis, the tests are strict. But then again, Goolam Panelbeaters can do miracles with cars, my dad says, especially old cars like his Dodge. Wide and long, it almost sails down the road, a bright red spaceship. He can beat them into shape. Wish he'd beaten me into shape for my tests, I think. Ha, fucking ha!

I blink back tears.

Failed. What does it mean?

We leave the car there.

Good riddance.

Salaam.

As we walk home, a deep silence comes down on us. A blanket of it. We don't say anything. My father is not one for words.

Then I say: 'Do you believe in god, Dad, you know, in the gods?' Not that I prayed much for a pass. But my mother sure did. Every day for the whole of my second year. Presenting offerings to every god you can think of.

He doesn't answer. We walk past the Lakavern roundabout, past the Assumption Church with the gory Jesus, down past the perfectly painted green and white Mosque, and he still hasn't answered.

When we get to the CNT bus depot, he says it: 'No.'

I don't say anything. But I feel a certain pride in him. Funny that. I never felt proud of him before.

That 'no' is like a nugget of truth. The only one I've got.

*

Home again.

Mum's still out at the shops. Thank god.

Failed. I try to suck the meaning out of the word. Like a pip between my teeth. But it's only got a *feeling*, this word. A feeling so low, so hopeless, so lonely, so inferior, so useless, so everything fucking awful, so guilty, yes, so guilty you want to give up.

So, I crouch on the back step with a mug of cold tea in my hand, hiding behind the columns of uneven ink of the

L'Express in front of me. That's the kind of thing I see: the ink.

The results have got to my gut lining too.

It aches.

I stare into the folds of the newspaper. Nothing in it. Just full of print. Until something catches my eye.

Je suis innocente. Wish I was.

Photograph of a girl. Blown up big from what must have been a snapshot taken as she was ushered into Court. Granular. *Stunted.* She looks stunted, like me. She's trying to hide her face. Same age as me. Shy. Scared.

Yesterday young girl . . . guilty drug trafficking. Maintains . . . Je suis innocente. Bombay Hotel, Bihari chambermaid. Boss gave her suitcase. Spices in it: 'Saffron. Fetches a good price.' Says she was given as a sample, a handful of red and yellow pistils, took them home to the flat she shared with eleven other hotel girls, soaked them in hot water to free the perfume, then cooked them in rice. Supposed to get two months' wages. What was in the suitcase turned out not saffron. At Customs . . . a search, dug a sharp knife into it, false bottom. Brown Sugar, the paper says. Sentence next week.

'They going to hang her?' Because you see I know about this. There was this debate about it at school: *Advantages and disadvantages of the death penalty.* The *advantages* won, even at school. Will she be the first one hanged?

Frightened girl, eyes of a mongoose in the middle of the motorway, a lorry heading for it full tilt.

Like me. *Failed.*

'*Crackdown on crime, war on drugs, stamp out the dealers, hang the merchants of death.*' The words come back to me now. My mum saying them when she got back from this do-gooders' meeting. The words just came babbling out of her. I put my fists in my ears, I can tell you.

And the very first victim this girl?

I feel dizzy now.

Eighteen, it says she is.

Par ailleurs, last one they hanged was called Alexandre, the newspaper reminds us. Had to hang him twice. Neck didn't break the first time. So it says.

The newspaper clouds over because of the prickle of self-pity in my eyes. I see the green snake of rope.

I turn the page. Very different photographs here. Clear as a bell. The bright colours of a car ad. New page, new world. Promising freedom. For just a few hundred thousand rupees.

Jardin d'un poste de police: Premier prix à Bambous. Flower garden awarded . . .

I fold the thing up.

'Ah, there you are,' she says, embarrassed, as she gets back from the shops, rustling parcels in both hands. 'Agh, never mind.'

She takes it well. Considering. Doesn't seem to mind one way or the other really. Does her pottering around. Funny, she is. She opens her mouth, starts saying something about Baya, but then she stops herself mid-sentence. Just hands me another cup of tea, a steaming cup of ginger tea, as if nothing untoward has happened. One of her words that, *untoward*. In passing, she just touches my cheek with the back of her hand. I shrug her off.

'Boy!'

'Mm.'

'Tell you what. Do me a favour. Here's some bus money for you.'

'What you mean, Ma?'

'You go on a mission for me?'

'You mean an errand, Mum?' I'm always correcting her English.

'You run an errand for me, Boy? Go see Mamu Dip and Renuka Mami. Mamu Dip's got a little something special for me. He'll give it to you to bring home to me. Later you go? A bit later, you get yourself ready, after you've finished your ginger tea and all. When you want to.' She's trying to make me forget it. She can't stand seeing my pain, me suffering before her eyes. *Mission*. Run an errand. Get me out of her sight.

But then.

I like Mamu Dip.

The only uncle I like. My mother's little brother. He lives in Krevker. Plants ginger. Harvests it. Their whole house smells of ginger.

And of garlic, too. They've got garlic tied up in bunches so thick, so close together it's a ceiling above the bed in the spare room. You should just see it. It's something, I tell you.

There's a mountain there, a huge mountain, just outside the back window. Or so it seems.

There's blue sky there. Wide open sky everywhere.

There's peace there, in their house, everything is calm. It's soothing. Gentle. Sweet. Kind. There. Not like here, where things rasp. Too full and yet empty. Too quiet and too noisy. Lonely.

Renuka Mami, I like her too. She's very young. I'm sorry she's already married to Mamu Dip, or I could have asked her to marry me. Silly, isn't it? I would like to marry someone like her. She's tall, strong and a bit wild. Lean as a deer on a mountainside. She goes picking wild pepper in the season, *red beads*, she calls it. She just tucks in her sari end, takes a gunny bag, and is off. She used to sell her wild peppercorns to Sarjua, then she started selling to Khaytoo.

'Karo Lalyann to Kat Born, how much? Kat Born to Porlwi, how much? Porlwi to Krevker, how much?' My mother's off again doing her calculations, all by herself, before I can even answer. She gets to take the bus much more than I do, and knows all the fares off by heart. Open market at Kat Born on Wednesdays, open market at Vakwa Thursdays. London Supermarket Fridays, Porlwi to see people in hospital, and then to a wedding here, a funeral there, and to birthday parties everywhere.

But, she has to do her sums out aloud. Otherwise, she might give me too much money, and I might go straight out and buy some sausage.

'There you are, an extra fifteen rupees so you can buy a loaf or two of bread for Renuka Mami at the Lagar Dinor. Will you go? For me? Your father's car is at Goolam Panelbeaters.' You wouldn't think I'd left it there myself.

'Is that too much to ask you to do for me? A mother and all? Do you agree to go then?'

'Yeah, Ma,' I say, 'I'll go.' For once she, in turn, knows what I'd like to do. For once.

Or is it me that's changing?

Baya and I used to stay over there. We were two younger brothers to him, to Mamu Dip, or sons. We three would go mountain climbing together. Baya and I would get up early, take the first CNT bus, the drivers' and conductors' bus, change at Porlwi, run across to the Lagar Dinor, buy a loaf of bread, get on to the first bus for Krevker. Then there, the three of us would criss-cross the fields together, hunting hare. You could hear our laughter resonating, I tell you.

It seems so long ago now, way back in my childhood. So

far away. In another lifetime. But one that is rising, like a wave of memory, and overwhelming me. A tidal wave, threatening to drown me.

I swallow.

I want to go. I want to go see Mamu Dip.

And get myself out of this house, go somewhere, any-where. Catch a bus, and go.

'But,' my mother continues, a radio she is, 'Why not stay overnight there? Or better still, why not stay two or three days, rather? Mamu Dip sent word that you're welcome. Says to stay over. Says you never stay over any more. Then, when you come back home, next week some time, don't you forget, you bring my little errand with you, and then, we'll see, you can go back to school again. Or we'll see.'

'Yes,' I say to her, 'Yes, I'd like that. I'll go. Right now, I'll go. Where's that bus money?'

'And take this pickle along will you? You give it to Renuka Mami. She loves *bilinbi*. Tell her I planted the bit of turmeric she gave me and it's doing well. And could you go pick a few lemons for your Mamu-uncle too? And I'll give you these curried chicken innards for him. He loves them and you know Mami is a bit vegetarian. That way, you can also get to eat some, in case you fade away without any meat for three or four days, Boy.' No doubt, she thinks I might be tempted to eat sausage. *Three or four days*, she says now. Good.

'What's the errand I have to bring for you then, Ma?'

'Your uncle will know. He asked me to send you to fetch it. Just a little something I need.'

Oh, *that*, I think.

I quickly think which religious service is due to come up. She, my mother, is the one who knows how to prepare the milk and the stuff and all the special spices that go with it,

21

especially for the men to drink, to make them sing better, to give body to the music, to make the gods come closer. *Bhang*, they call it. When you hear them singing, you can believe it.

Oh yes, of course. It's Granbasin. The Granbasin festival comes at around results time. The suicide reports are always in the same newspapers as photographs of beautiful bamboo *kanwarr* full of paper flowers balancing on men's shoulders, men going to fetch holy water from the Ganges. Well not exactly the Ganges, but better. From a deep and mysterious lake. *Gran Basin*.

Reflected in that lake, I see the granular photograph of the girl from India. In its waters. She too, sent on an errand.

My mother, I have to tell you, knows how to make all sorts of preparations. Not everyone knows these things. She learnt when her grandfather had his *Gannja ke Dukann*. That was in Krevker too. Had a licence to sell alcohol and the leaves of tobacco and marijuana.

That's also why Mamu Dip's friends have given him the nickname '*Interline Cropper*'. Supposedly he only plants ginger *interline*, relative to that other more lucrative now illegal crop.

*

For five whole minutes, I have forgotten my exams and my results. Mamu Dip can do that for you, he can. He's like a magician that way. When you think about him, you feel happy. He's got *a taste for the good things in life*, he has, which is why it's been so hard to go and stay with him without Baya.

I take the basket and hang it around my neck. It's quite tall for a lemon tree, and you have to watch out for the thorns. Not that I'd care if I got a fucking crown of them.

I hear a pair of turtledoves cooing above me. This makes me move without making a sound. When I get to where they are, I look into their nest. The two of them are sitting there right on top of their baby turtledove-chick. In case anything happens to it. And you should see the rubbishy nest they've made. Full of too much straw. Sitting right on top of their chick, as though he's still an egg.

But suddenly, there's this perfume. Just from one lone late lemon flower. It hits me. I could swoon, I swear it, it's so perfect, that smell. I try to catch it inside my nose, and hold it.

I pick a first lemon, and look at it. On an impulse, I bite into its skin. Bitter. I peel the whole thing with my teeth, and then eat it. Just like that. Without salt or chilli or anything. In the open air. Wow!

'Why you just sitting up there like that, Boy?' My mother stares up at me in the lemon tree.

'Just thinking,' I reply.

'Just thinking, hey? From nursery school you've been like that. Baya wasn't like that when he was little. He was . . . Now, don't go thinking too much about your exams, then.'

She doesn't use the word 'results'. I appreciate that.

All at once, while I'm sitting up that lemon tree, I think how difficult it must be for *her*. Now that there's just me. I'm the *other* son. The one who can't do anything right. The *boy*.

My Baya. He also loved *bilinbi* pickle.

*

I go into my room quietly, close the door behind me, and lean on it. I run the fingers of both my hands over the peeling-off paint. I hear my own breathing.

So anyway I do it. I go over to the metal trunk, pull it away from the wall, and open its lid. Only mustiness. Everything is folded neatly. Untouched. I let my hand feel the comb he kept in his pocket, his door key, his wallet, his compass, the bangle with his name engraved on it, Balmick Burton. Piles of this and that. Then I see them. Wrapped in red and yellow kite-making paper, just peeping out. His running shoes. His navy-blue smart running shoes.

That's what he'd like me to have. I know it.

'They'll be too big,' I say to myself. And I'm about to look for something else instead, when I decide to just try one on.

I would never have believed it.

Perfect fit.

So I take out the other one and close up the trunk again.

Then, I have this afterthought and I open it again, and take out the bangle too. Good luck charm.

First thing my mother says is: 'Oh! Look how nice your Baya's running shoes look on you!'

I feel exposed. Naked and sore.

In her voice, is it pleasure, or resentment? Is it congratulations or an accusation? Surprise or sorrow?

How would I know?

I'm flustered.

Fucking hell.

So I just kiss them both goodbye, promise I won't do anything *untoward*, her word, *untoward*. I think to myself 'especially not eat sausages'.

So that is how I turn my back on my parents and leave.

Like I'm gonna jump off the high diving board, I can tell you.

I step out.

Over my shoulder, my denim bag.

Funny thing happens to me out in the street. *Lanbeli. Akalmi.* A sort of calmness comes down on me. And there are these strange words singing loud in my ears and in my heart: '*Peace! It comes with freedom*'. I can't find the meaning to these sounds. I just hear the song. The feeling. The vibrations of the notes.

Ridiculous, but there it is.

'*Peace! It comes with freedom*'.

*

And that's when I start doing things I never do.

First, instead of catching a bus like I'm supposed to, to the Kat Born bus station, I *walk* there.

I *walk* to the Kat Born bus station.

Walk. Funny. Even suspicious, that. Most odd. In my Baya's running shoes.

Not that it's that far. It isn't.

Nor that it's not good for me. It is. I need exercise after two years of preparing for exams. And the walk might shake the word *fail* out of my hair.

Baya, he used to walk everywhere, he did. Sometimes he would take me. Or let me tag along.

I look down at the navy-blue running shoes without thinking.

As though he's left a kind of vacuum in the big wide world, and I am being drawn into it, to fill it up? The call of it.

But there's a more practical thing, too. I get to keep the bus money.

Yes, I get to keep the money in case I need it later, you never know. I'm not dingthrifty. Another one of her words that, *dingthrifty*. Baya and I would laugh. Where d'you get that word from, Ma? *Dingthrifty*. 'I don't want my sons dingthrifty,' she would say. In the singular now, *my son dingthrifty*. I pocket the money. *Just in case*.

For me, this amounts to a lie. An untruth. A mendacity. A false statement under oath. A bearing of false witness. So after swearing, I'm beginning now to start *lying*. Slippery slope. And is it *stealing* too?

I'll be left with money that isn't mine. This logic, childish as it is, is all I've got. It represents a kind of honesty to me. My mother expects it of me that I be on the bus, therefore, on the bus I must be.

But not today. Today is different.

Before today, I've never slept outside my parents' house. Today will be the first time. Well, the first time I'll have done it *on my own*. Baya and I slept at relatives' houses any time we wanted to. We stayed at Mamu Dip's seven times in all. Seven.

Funny thing that. Baya used to sleep all over the place. For nothing. On his own. At this one's house, or at the other one's place. Camping in a tent, or renting a bungalow at Pereber. Or putting up a square of tarpaulin at Lapreri. Where people are always getting drowned it's so dangerous. Right there.

*

As I am going down the Kandos hill, I just look up, you know, for nothing. And what do I see? I see coming towards me *her*. A girl. The most beautiful. Eyes, as if she just saw the world. For the first time. Calm and alive, those eyes. And her mouth. Relaxed, full. Her neck poised as she walks. Her eyes meet mine, and they stay met. Oh, my god. What am I going to do?

She is walking up the hill. Her hair lifts up from her neck as she walks. That's how I can see her neck. Her hair gently bounces. But it's her eyes. A million colours of brown in them. She is still looking right into my eyes. She smiles, languid. She walks up the hill with more ease than I am walking down it. At the closest point, I can almost touch her.

I wait until she has gone right past before turning around to watch her. Her dress is tight around her waist and on her hips. Then it flares out, undulating as she walks. Maybe she has just passed her exams. Then she stops, this girl does, quite suddenly, her two perfect feet each in a perfect walking shoe. She is staring at hand-painted posters stuck up on the outside wall of the Telecom building. I strain to read them: 'Don't sell off the people's jewels!' What 'people's jewels'? She does a funny thing then, the girl. She goes up to the wall and touches one of the posters. A caress. Then she walks on up the hill. And I find myself being carried down the hill faster now.

A-spin.

As I go past the Kandos hospital gate, a bit further down the hill, I see *another* poster: 'Don't privatize hospital catering!' The texture of the hand-painted letters makes me want to touch it too.

Then there's the mortuary. Squatting there. Do you

think the word *mortuary* sounds less dead than the word *morgue*? I don't know.

Maybe there will be a young person laid out in the morgue soon. Exam results bring a crop of suicides. That's what they call it. A crop.

'Be selling *that* off soon, too, the morgue,' I joke to myself, 'Then you'd have to pay to get in there.' I imagine myself making this joke to her.

So I end up laughing as I go down the hill past the mortuary.

My denim bag bounces on my shoulder. In it, a spare T-shirt and underpants, a toothbrush, the bangle with Balmick Burton engraved on it. Uncle Dip will lend me a pair of sponge flip-flops and Renuka Mami will give me a towel to use. And there's the *bilinbi* pickle, a dozen lemons, and a glass Ricoffy jar stuffed full of curried chicken innards. I quickly swing the bag off my shoulder and check its yellow lid is screwed on tightly. Even though the whole thing's in a plastic bag. Imagine if it all spilt out in the bus. I would die of shame.

I've also got a fern in another plastic bag inside my denim bag. That's for Renuka Mami. She adores ferns. I chose one of those with black stems, shiny black stems, and bright green little leaves. Ferns are sensitive things, they say, and yet my mother manages to grow them. Makes you think. Anyway, Renuka Mami will love it. Any fern would grow under her hand.

Past the CD shop in Lalwiz. Look into the window. I would like that new Michael Jackson. Now *he* can sing. And he can dance. I can't do either. And yet he looks so miserable most of the time. As miserable as me. That high-pitched shriek he lets out between the words in his

songs, it echoes in my heart somewhere. Do you pick
that up?

*

At the Lagar Dinor naturally I go to the chilli-cake seller,
where she sits, firmly over there on a wooden box, like
the conductor of an orchestra, only sitting, poking
rhythmically with one hand at this cake then that one
in the sizzling oil in front of her, and firmly tucking in
her blue and mauve sari-end, like she's turning the page
of the score, with the other. Not that I know that much
about orchestras. I ask for three rupees worth. For
Mamu Dip and Renuka Mami, with part of the bus
money I've saved. It's the only place you can get chilli
cakes with holes in the middle. She serves me with
ceremony, slipping the cakes into a white paper packet.
'Your change, young man!'

Hear that. *Young man.*

'Life is looking up,' I mumble to myself.

Then I look around for the man who sells the big loaves
of bread. In Krevker you only get bread rolls, so I have to
buy a big loaf of bread. I look all around the bus station,
but I can't see the bread seller anywhere.

I almost feel panic. Disappeared? And my mother said I
have to buy a loaf of bread.

Funny that. I notice something. There are only three
street merchants today? Where are they all gone? I pluck
up my courage and ask the woman I bought the chilli
cakes from. She sits there, legs astride, stirring the cakes

29

with her skewer and keeping an eye open on the whole station.

'The loaves-of-bread man, where's he gone, please?'

'Police,' she says, pushing the strands back with her *horni*.

I can't believe what she's saying.

'Police chase us away!' She looks away from me, even. Pulls her *horni* down over her head now, in a gesture of defiance.

Oh my god, the things I don't know.

So, I put my denim bag down between my feet, and stand there. I've got the time, so I might as well listen to her. If she wants to say anything, that is. Sort of let the world into me. For once.

'Don't know why, but they hound us out,' she curses. 'No one gets to take loaves of bread to their families in the north any more.' I still just stand there, so she goes on. 'And at night, it's haunted now. A bus station gone spooky, without any street merchants. Look now, see how on edge I am? Just waiting for someone to shout "Watch out! Piroké!" and I grab all my things and run. Not easy with boiling oil, I can tell you.'

'Who's Piroké?' I am terrified already of Piroké. The way she spits out his name.

'Not like it used to be around here. Piroké? He's the chief CID man. You know something? Your bread seller. His father sold bread here before him, and his father's father, before *him*. Under that same big bannwar tree. Night and day, the family sold bread. An *institution*.' She mulls over this word.

'An *institution*. A form of happiness for everyone. Like my mother before me cooked and sold these same cakes right here.' She points to the ground with the skewer.

'With the holes in them, too.' She slips one up her skewer to show me. 'Now the authorities have chased him away. Creating disorder where there was order. They'll be cutting the big bannwar tree down soon. So I hear. I'm stubborn. I stay. I know they don't want to look ugly, beating up a woman in public, so I stay. And there's the hot oil.' She puts her head back, way back, and at first I don't know what's happening. Then I realize she's laughing. She's laughing so hard, she doubles forwards again. Yeah, there's hot oil, I think. She points at the earth again, claiming it, with her skewer. Then with the end of her sari, she wipes tears from her eyes. Laughter, crying, oil smoke?

'I'm sorry,' I mumble.

'Not much use you being sorry, young man,' she replies. Her eyes are dry again now.

'True, it's not much use, is it?' I indeed am not much use to anyone at all.

I pick up my bag, head bowed now, and go over to the man selling tapioca cakes. They are on the front of his bicycle in a smart glass box. For fast getaways. So translucent, the cakes are, made in perfect squares, sprinkled with grated fresh coconut so they don't stick to one another, piled in a pyramid, so I buy two rupees worth from him. He puts them in a square bag made out of old newspaper, which, together with the chilli cakes, I shove down into my denim bag. Next to the chicken innards.

I've still got some money left, from walking the first leg and from not getting the big loaf of bread. This pleases me, for some reason. Like I'm a felon.

Bus conductors hang out of bus doors, yelling for passengers to different destinations. Drivers, glitter and tinsel in their cabins, hoot to attract attention. I go across to my bus. The conductor sings out: *Krevker, Montayn*

Long. Squeezing past him, I get on to the bus and find a window seat. A peanut seller goes through the waiting bus. ''*Stas sale. 'Stas bwi.*' A woman beggar follows, 'Give me a rupee or two, sir, madam. How old would you take me for, sir?' She looks at me. *Sir.* Now I'm an expert on age? Her hair's all fallen out. She is tiny, her voice the voice of a child. But her face is seventy years old. Her ears big against it, like great great granny's. Skin dry as Bombay duck. Eyes old, old, old. Looking at me. 'Don't deceive me with your kindness, sir.' 'Take no notice of her,' a lottery seller follows close behind her, shoving her along. All his tickets are displayed miraculously green, their numbers vying to look lucky, clothes pegs fastening them down to a sheet of cardboard dangling from a string around his neck. 'Friday. Friday!' like he's selling Fridays. 'Friday draw day. Maybe your day. Never know! Never know! Lady Luck may just be stalking your back yard? Draw day, your day. *Destiny's day.* A *millionaire*, the word is written on your own forehead. Just here!' He pulls three fingers across his brow, and laughs aloud. Passengers proffer coins, grab green bits of paper. And a newspaper vendor follows close behind him, 'Diagonal!' The word catches my ear. 'Diagonal! Finance Minister talks eyewash. News! News! Prime Minister furious. Politics goes diagonal!'

I see the paper, the blade slitting, splitting it, diagonal. Now '*politics goes diagonal*'.

I laugh out the bus window. I can't help it.

Out of the bus window, I see two, no, three young men, thin as rakes, go into the public toilets. Busy, busy, busy. Hurry, hurry, hurry. Drugs, I think. Drugs, drugs, drugs. Their lives full of incessantly, pressingly urgent events. *Trasé, trasé, trasé.*

While a woman, slow in her brown uniform from the

Private Cleaners' Company, drapes her arm over her mop by the women's toilets, observing. She smiles. Now she gossips with another woman in brown. They are not in any hurry. Time is something else for them. A very female thing. That goes round and round and round. Something boys and men don't know about.

A group of four or five Taiwanese and South Korean sailors waddle-walk right under the bus window. Their feet mourning the roll of the sea. Consternation in them. Then I hear the words 'Tru Fanfaron'. I hear the word 'pickpocket'. I watch them walk towards the Tru Fanfaron police station. I see them preparing a formal complaint. They've been robbed. Two of them no more than my age. That's for sure. So far away from home?

While rowdy young lorry helpers from the lorry stand sit under the other big bannwar tree, minding other people's business, spreading rumours, and preparing to go distribute new slang words around the country to-gether with the merchandise they deliver. That's what my teacher said. It's them that carry *language* around. How would we all speak the same without them, he asked the class?

I am still left speechless by this question.

*

When the road turns in at the junction and goes towards Montayn Long, the bus itself relaxes its muscles. You can't believe it. A sort of slowness, and deep breathing sets in. The vehicle calms down. Stops hooting for nothing. It doesn't even rev up for nothing any more either, nor brake sharply after accelerating too much. Nor is there much traffic left on the Branch Road anyway.

Passengers begin to talk to the person who has been sitting next to them in silence all the way so far. *'Water's going up, I don't know how I'm going to manage,'* and *'I hear the Minister had a hard time at the meeting in your street,'* and *'Your niece from Lalmati, the fair one with short hair, I happen to know a boy from a very nice family.'*

No more hurry. No more bustle. Life settles down to the rhythm of the countryside. Over just those few miles? Peace, tranquillity.

'Don't sentimentalize, Krish,' I say to myself, 'Only rural idiocy you're seeing.'

But the mountain draws nearer, too.

It's a fact.

Slowly but surely, bus stop by bus stop. Giving me its different faces as the road winds this way and that. The caring aunt mountain, the fierce mother mountain, the flippant young girl mountain, the scary devil mountain, the hesitant boy mountain, the cold indifferent father mountain, the cross goddess mountain, the innocent bystander mountain, the embracing lover mountain. The sky here, it's so clear it hurts. The sun passes overhead so low here, I should have brought a cap. Sugar cane gives way to ginger plants, whose pointed leaves coil around into a fine point. Flat lands give way to the foothills of the mountain.

So I pull the string and ring the bell. Get off the bus, cross the road, and watch all the airborne seeds flying across the road in the air just next to my face. Multiplying. And two yellow and brown queen-of-the-oceans giant butterflies hide their colours, then show them, hide their colours, then show them.

Is this side, the other side of the road, better?

How would I know?

As I'm bending over like that to tie the laces of one of Baya's navy-blue running shoes, and as I'm leaning over to put my denim bag down on a big rock next to the return bus stop, my eye gets caught by a ladybird. A tiny ladybird sitting on the rock. I stop in midair. All on its own. A self-contained, self-possessed, dignified creature. Shiny black with red spots. Could I be like that? Whole? Is the world like this every day? Are there butterflies and ladybirds and flying seeds? Do I only see these things now? I bend over and look at the ladybird. I *love* that ladybird, such a calm creature, so you know what I do? I wish it a pleasant day, and instead of putting my bag down next to it – it would be such a big thing to have next to her – I just flip the bag over my shoulder, and sit down on my haunches to tie my shoelace. Then I turn away from the ladybird and go straight towards Mamu Dip and Renuka Mami's house. Full stride.

So, maybe. Or, maybe.

Maybe I *have* got a life ahead of me.

Out there. Like a road opening out towards something. A future. I don't know how it comes about, but when I get there, as I am crossing that road, even before I saw that ladybird, I earned a kind of calm. I feel I *earned* it. It's *that* that made me see the ladybird.

The mountain smiles at me then. I see it.

I say to myself, 'What a load of rubbish, Boy!'

But. But it's as if I have broken some chain. And a rich swelling outwards of pleasure comes with being alive. Is this a beginning? Can I take the risk?

Beginning of what I can't tell you. I don't know myself. But a beginning?

*

Denim bag on shoulder, and with that stride, it takes me no more than a minute to get to Mamu Dip and Renuka Mami's front yard, and I find myself stepping under the two enormous, gnarled old mango trees that throw a thick dark-green hug of shade over me and over the whole wooden slatted roof of their house. The enchanted house. I am being drawn in. They haven't got a gate. You walk in, just like that.

And there they are, walking out, arms open. Mamu Dip's huge black handlebar moustache, Renuka Mami's soft-flowing red *horni* with gold threadlets shining in the dark shade, running to keep up. Running towards me. Together, they make up the ladybird.

I smell the heady perfume of the frangipani in front of their door. And I remember Baya and me late at night, smelling it as it came through the open wooden bedroom window. He leant out and picked a flower one night – white, turning yellow towards the middle, and then this sudden bright pink right in the centre – and, holding it by its stem, spun it round like a propeller between his forefinger and his thumb. And the perfume of that one blossom filled the bedroom.

'Heard about your results, I did,' Mamu Dip says at once, as he swoops down to kiss my cheek, his moustache also bending down, tickling me. Now I smell his pipe tobacco in his pocket, and I could cry. 'Well they're over, son. Over and done with.' He leaves no embarrassing moment, when I would have to fill in things. Just comes out with it. So easy. *Over and done with.* A feeling of relief comes over me, just like the thick shade of those two ancient mango trees. A hug. And no gate. The delicate perfumes of frangipani and pipe tobacco all around me.

'Failed,' I say, 'I have failed.'

'Why d'you have to say *failed*? Not a very useful word, that. Ah! Throw it away, will you! Life is not just pass and fail, you know!' He laughs loudly, and with disrespect, loudly and I don't know what at. 'Why not try saying "I didn't pass" instead? You could say that, couldn't you now? Keep everybody happy, that.'

Renuka Mami laughs too, tucking in the strands, looking at him adoringly. She thinks his jokes hilarious. I find myself laughing more. They make exams seem faraway, ludicrous things, they do.

'T'hell with exams!' he says. 'Let's talk about other things. What did your Ma put into your little bag for me? My big sister always sends something special for her little brother, that I know.' With this, he grabs me towards him, hugs me close to his big tummy, and just holds me like that, really hard for a while, my breathing knocked right out of me. I relax, and let him hold me, and breathe in the smell of pipe tobacco. Then he loosens his grip, and does a sort of mock waltz. One-two-three. One-two-three. And pretends to signal a hello to some vague acquaintance of his sitting on the edge of the dance floor. And we all laugh again. Ballroom dancing being the funniest thing we've ever heard of.

'Renuka Mami, a fern especially for you.' I have to give her hers first because she's the in-law. She grabs my head and kisses me on both cheeks, and then on my lips. I could faint. She looks at the fern, at its shiny black stems, with such love. Then, she bends down and hugs me tight around the knees, and I don't know what she's going to do, and then she picks me up right into the air. That's how strong she is. That's my aunt for you. So, when she puts me down, I pick her up into the air the same way. An aunt! Then we collapse laughing, as if we've invented a new step in the ballroom dancing. Mamu Dip, not to be outdone, comes and lifts us both up at once, one in each arm. Hanuman. And does a prance under the mango tree, and then swings us both around so our legs fly outwards.

There are people like that. Look at Renuka Mami. A fern, a silly old fern left over from the ice age, can make her so happy she could cry. I would love to be like that. Imagine if a fern could make me happy. I hand her the chilli cakes, too, and apologize about no loaf of bread, the man wasn't there selling bread, I say. Concern blows over her eyebrows. She seems to take note of that phrase. Then I hand her the little bag made out of old newspaper and she knows it's full of tapioca cakes. She holds them to her face, smelling the vanilla perfume coming through the bag. I hadn't even noticed the smell when I bought them.

'Thank god no fern for me. It's not edible enough!' Mamu Dip knows the kind of thing his big sister will send him.

He can probably guess what's in my bag without even looking. Guess the *bilinbi* pickle. Guess the chicken innards curry in a jar, guess a dozen lemons. But, when he actually sees them, he is overcome with joy as if it is a total surprise to him, something he never dreamt of.

He takes his presents into the house in strides.

Then I'm lost in the ferns. All around the bases of the

two mango trees in pots and jars, and hanging in tins from nails in the trees, and in plastic jars balancing on every nook and cranny in each joint of each branch of each tree up to where you can reach, there are ferns, ferns, ferns. Small, lacy-green ferns spilling 360 degrees around milk tins all over the place. Breathing cool. Giant ferns with outrageous fronds in barrels cut in half, here and there. Left over from the beginning of time. Delicate, narrow-leafed pale-green ferns competing for space. Deep bottle-green ferns, green green green in that dark shade. Fluffy, spidery, curly ferns. Austere upright ferns.

*

I don't know how the confusion comes about.

Everything gets mixed up real fast, and then it all settles down and jells, all upside down, even faster. Totally harmless, like. It all happens in a matter of minutes. Then it's like it's irreversible. Fixed. Destiny has done what it's had to do and it's done. Can't be undone. And nothing can be done about it now. And it doesn't really matter anyway. Or so it seems to me.

This is what happens.

Mamu Dip says he's going out fishing, fishing 'beyond the reef', he says, with a friend of his from Granbe in one of those high-bowed, big heavy wooden sail-pirogues that go way out to ply the deep-sea fishing banks, the banks that are underwater continents. Do I want to come along, he asks? Now, the error is about to happen. I somehow can't manage to say 'yes'. This is for all sorts of reasons, but what happens is that I hesitate. I don't say 'yes' fast enough for Mamu Dip. And I don't have a simple 'no' answer ready either. I like fishing too much, I like Mamu Dip too much, I'm dying to say 'yes' too much to be able to say 'no'.

But I should have said 'no'. A complicated 'no' if need be. I haven't brought seasick pills, but then what if he says he's got some. I've never been beyond the reef. Even inside the lagoon at Rivyer Nwar, when Baya and I went out in a small pirogue, I got seasick. So, I start to stutter instead. The words st-stu-stutter along. And I start to blunder. Probably it's because I want to say 'yes', but I'm too scared to say 'yes'. Or I express myself poorly, or I am ashamed of getting seasick. 'No, I won't be c-c-coming. I've got to g-go back home straight away.' I hear myself say the words: 'I've got to get back t-t-today.' I just made it up. A lie.

'I can't believe it,' Renuka Mami gasps. 'Today? But, why? What are you telling me? I can't bear it. It can't be true. Go on, stay. Change your mind. Whatever's the matter with you? Is the food not good enough here for you then?'

She half-thinks I'm teasing, so she teases back.

And I just go and get into deeper water: 'Four o'clock,' I reply, 'I have something important to g-g-get done . . . at home. I'll have to leave at four o'clock.'

'But I sent word to your mother, I told her . . .' Mamu Dip goes on. They are very good at this 'sending word' to one another. 'She said, she said . . .'

And now real lies start to get into it. I know I'm not expected home. I'm not even supposed to be home by midnight. I've got four days here. No way I have to be back. I know this full well. Where did I get this four o'clock thing? And so I launch into inventing what it is I

40

have to do at four o'clock. And I don't even stutter any more. It comes out all formal, too.

'Yes. They are expecting me back today. I have informed them that I shall be leaving here in the vicinity of four o'clock. I have things to look into at home. Concerning the question of when I shall be going back to school. Getting a place sorted out. And other important business matters.' What a mouthful.

Renuka Mami protests. But Mamu Dip listens to me closely, mulls things over quietly to himself, no doubt shocked by the good grammar, and then replies: 'Next time, then. You stay over next time,' he says, probably noticing my stuttering and then non-stuttering, 'because we have to go up Piter Bot Mountain, you and I. Is that a deal, then?' He is not a man to force someone to do something he doesn't seem to want to do. He just leaves it up to me. Does he know it's the seasickness, that's why he mentions the mountains? Does he pick up the funny feelings I'm having? He knows I shouldn't be forced. So, he just says: 'Let the child be, Eho. Jayde. Let him be. It'll pass.' Whatever it is, he means, it'll pass.

Up to this point, I haven't got any bad intentions. I haven't got any intentions at all. I swear it.

It's just a *misunderstanding*. Could have happened to anyone.

Exam stress. Results upset me. I don't know.

'As for me, I'm off fishing now then,' Mamu Dip announces after lunch. He gets up, hugs me, says: 'And, so that I don't forget, there's this too! This little not-to-be-forgotten thingamabob.' There and then, he walks over to his table, pulls out a drawer, and picks up a tiny little seethrough cellophane packet twisted at the top and says, 'Here's the stuff for your mother, then. You know what it is. Beware, my son. Beware. You know what the police are like these days. *Cross as wasps.* Grab people's relatives and lock them up for nothing. Now, look after this errand well, then. Push it way down into your trouser pocket, see?' He puts pressure on the tiny bit of transparent cigarette cellophane with the special twist that compresses the grass, and he presses it into the palm of my hand.

And so my errand begins.

I am an errand bearer now. Bearing an errand between a man and his sister, for the gods. Errand-boy. Commissioned. A young man with a commission. A mission. I am an ambassador. Taking messages from the head of state of one country to that of another.

And Uncle Dip goes off fishing, happy in having delegated his nephew to do the errand. My mother happy at home that I am on this mission.

*

Renuka Mami and I spend a quiet afternoon together. She walks me around her fruit trees, pointing out the different kinds of ferns that grow in their shade-producing cool, in that hot afternoon, saying who gave her which one, and which one she gave a bit of to who else. We walk under the avocado trees whose branches have grown droopy with the weight of the fruit they're bearing, the orange tree, the huge big-leafed breadfruit tree decorated with its enormous pale-green balls with tiny hexagons all over its skin. Granadilla trellises link parts of the garden to each other, a cluster of banana trees produces wildly, giant leaves, red flowers, huge branches of bananas, and under a custard apple tree rich with leaves we sit on a wooden bench and look at the soursop hanging big and prehistoric from the branches of the next tree along. Then she gets up and climbs up one of the giant mango trees to find me a late mango. Then she peels it for me, cuts it into bits.

I could forget anything when I'm with her.

Then we go back on to the verandah and I ask her to tell me a story like she used to when Baya and I were little. She goes and picks up the old notebook she keeps all her stories written down in, and walks over to grandfather's cane chair with its armrests, and curls her feet up on it under her skirt. She half-reads, half-tells me a story, while I sit on the doorstep between verandah and house. There are straw blinds adding to the coolness. 'Why don't other people write down stories like you do, Renuka Mami?' I ask.

'They've got better memories than me, maybe, so they don't need to write them down,' she laughs.

'There's this woman,' she says. And her story goes on. 'She used to live . . .'

Renuka Mami puts her head back and laughs at the end of her story. But I am disturbed. The story scares me. 'What's the matter, then?' Renuka Mami asks me. 'The story,' I say, 'It's got so many morals, and no morals.'

'It's only a story, Krish,' she says, 'only a story.'

She knows I like puffy banana fritters and sweet potato cakes shaped like envelopes, so that's what she fries to go with our tea.

'Next time, you stay over,' she says, 'honey.'

She's the one who's a honey, I can tell you that.

I kiss her goodbye.

43

And instead of feeling sad, I find in myself a kind of eagerness to set off.

Funny that.

*

As soon as I start walking back to the bus stop, I remember my ladybird on the rock. I hurry over. But it has flown away. Obviously. *Ladybird, ladybird, fly away home, your house is on fire, your children will burn.* Ladybirds are like that. They don't sit around. They've got responsibilities. But while I am still looking for it, I say to myself in a voice that's a bit like Baya's: 'Anyone would give anything to have an uncle like that. Couldn't you have gone fishing with him? What's the matter with you then? Need your head read?'

I don't give myself any answer. In case I start stuttering again.

Then to myself I reply, 'Maybe next time. Maybe next time.'

Meanwhile, I have seen, opening up before me, one, two or three, maybe even *three or four*, free days, whole days free, free ahead of me. Before my very eyes.

I look down at the running shoes I'm wearing. They seem to be raring to go. Then up again at the big wide world.

The whole future opens up before my eyes.

I see the bus getting nearer. And in no time, there I am climbing in, just as I should be. It's full, so I weave my way between standing passengers clustered at the front of the bus. Stupid that, the way they all stand in the front like that. I go to the second last row at the back of the bus, where there are two seats free, and I take up the window seat. No one is sitting next to me. Maybe they prefer standing in a clump in the front to sitting right at the back because of the bumps. Others are moving forward on their way to the front to get out at one of the next stops.

And so, the bus chugs along. The bus conductor never seems to get a chance to get to me because at every bus stop some people get off and other new people get on and find places to sit nearer the front, and he looks after them first. By the time we get to Montayn Long, the bus is sardine packed, and a policeman, bulging out of his uniform, winds his hefty way to the back of the bus, and plonks himself down next to me. Oouf! He puts his feet out in front of him, loosens his belt, tilts his policeman's hat down slightly, lets out a loud burp, and closes his eyes.

Disgusting, I think to myself, and move a few inches away from him.

'Been stuffing himself someplace,' I think cruelly, 'No doubt bribery. Whisky and grilled seafood.' I don't know, maybe it's unfair of me.

Then I forget about him. I lift up into the clouds. Dreaming away out the window, scenery skimming past. *Three or four days. Not three or four hours.* I see myself riding a horse bareback in an open field. I see myself lying on my back eating a toffee apple, the sweet and the sour shocking my taste buds. I see myself kneeling down, rinsing my hair at a crystal clear spring, and shaking my head so that water drops fly in all directions. My face blue like Krishna's. And the girl, I see her hips moving, the girl from Kandos. And I see myself running in a wide space, wearing my Baya's running shoes.

'Fares,' the bus conductor says, 'All fares.' He doesn't take money from the policeman because they travel free. They get their travelling money from the government and then they travel free as well. Even *I* know that. I'm busy getting back to thinking about his burping, his free travel, his free whisky and seafood, when the conductor puts his hand out to me. I dive into my trouser pocket to get out my money.

But my fingers bump into something hard and oval-shaped that I don't seem to recognize the feel of, deep down in my pocket. I decide to fish it out and see what it is, and just as I get it out into the open there, in the palm of my right hand, at that very moment, I remember what it is, and freeze: the measure of grass rolled up in cellophane with the end twisted round. A *puliah*. Cannabis. My errand from Mamu Dip to my mother. For the Granbasin service. Errant me. Error-making me. Errand boy. Fool's errand.

Some god, please, save me.

The bus conductor looks up at the sky, as if to say what kind of a freak is this anyway in my bus, what kind of fool. *Dernye gopya*, he mouths. Then he looks at the policeman with a behind-the-back-of-the-teacher look to me, and I hear him mumbling, 'Fucking screw loose,' and looking in my direction. Instead of turning the handle of his ticket machine, he turns his hand around his own head, implying I'm off my head.

I am.

The policeman is transfixed. Maybe he's drunk. Or just blanked out. His eyes are open, but stare absent-mindedly into space, focused about two foot ahead of him. That's luck for you. Most likely he's got this act so that he doesn't have to pay and at the same time he doesn't even have to negotiate not to. Thinking his own thoughts, he is, self-importantly. Not paying a blind bit of attention to us. Thank you, god. Whichever one. The god of fucking screws loose. The god of good luck charms. The god of Baya's bracelet. The god of messenger boys.

My heart starts beating again. And I get my money out and pay: 'Branch Road, please. Just to the Branch Road. The junction.'

The conductor gives me my ticket, laughs at me heartily and says aloud, 'Talk about being a silly jerk. What's in your skull then? Prawn shit? Need your head read.'

But, meanwhile, I have already said the magic words: 'Just to the Branch Road, please!' And I don't even know why I said them. 'Junction.'

And at the very same time, I realize I nearly got *busted* and I never even used the word before. And suddenly I see her again, the girl from India. She must have made some mistake that made them stab that suitcase bottom. The god of little mistakes deserted her. And they busted her.

*

'You know something,' I say to myself when I get off the bus – I'm so slow, it's only just really sinking in – 'Mum and Dad are expecting me in *three or four days' time*. And Mamu Dip and Renuka Mami have sent me home already today. Do you realize what this means? Three or four days' surplus in my calendar. Free. Three or four days' pure freedom. All to myself. What should I do with them, then?'

No one to give me advice.

So, that is how it comes to pass that I decide to keep another leg of transport money, so I can add it to the money left from the first leg which I walked, and from the loaves of bread which I *didn't* buy at the Lagar Dinor because the bread seller had been chased away by the police.

I decide to hitchhike.

I get the idea there and then. On the spot. *I'll hitch a lift.* To stock a bit more cash up.

I, Krish, alias Boy, will hitch a ride. The words sound like music to my ears. *Hitch a ride.*

'Impossible,' I think to myself. I look at my body. I feel like a shrimp. Then I say it out aloud. 'I'll hitchhike.'

'It's *people* who hitchhike, Krish,' I say to myself, 'And it's *people* who will stop and give them a lift.'

Snarky.

One simple decision left, now that I'm free: which side of the road should I stand on? In which direction would I like to go? Practical issue. Towards Porlwi, I think. Only keep my money, not change my direction.

Or, on the other hand, should I rather go in the opposite direction?

Why not go north then? Possibilities open up all around me.

'Shall I head north then?' I ask myself. And I wonder which way my Baya would have gone.

No. To Porlwi, as planned.

Which is how I start hitchhiking. Just to get a bit of loose cash. That's all. I haven't got any other intention. I promise. On my honour. Hope to die.

I stand underneath the billboard with a big ad for mobile phones, with my denim bag over my shoulder, and as the first car goes by, I raise my hand into the air, just like I've seen people doing in films.

I say aloud to myself: 'There you go, Krish, there you go!'

When cars whiz by, not stopping, I say, 'It's patience that cures veldsores, Krish, patience that cures veldsores.'

*

I should have put more thought into it, I shouldn't have been so impulsive, I should have hesitated the way I usually do, but I just went ahead, I just went right ahead and hitchhiked. I should at least have predicted that what would stop in front of me, when it stopped, would most likely, nine out of ten chances, be none other than a *car*. And I should have at least remembered that one thing I hate is cars. I could have at least remembered that.

Before jumping in boots and all. Baya's running shoes and all, to be more precise.

But I didn't give it a thought.

'Direct action, Krish, there you go,' I say to myself.

Just standing there, thumb in the air, at the Branch Road Junction, in my T-shirt and jeans, in my Baya's navy-blue running shoes, floppy denim bag over my shoulder, no more than a spare T-shirt and underpants in it, and a toothbrush. And my Baya's old bangle with his name etched on to it. And in my trouser pocket, I get a chill of fright again, there it snuggles, the errand from Mamu Dip to my mother, an errand in my pocket. The policeman didn't notice it at all when I pulled it out, so he didn't grab me and lock me up. My luck held. And I've got a couple of rupees extra rattling in my pocket, too.

49

As I'm standing there, staring into space, first dozens and then hundreds of young women suddenly appear before me. Like they came out the ground. Where were they before? Some of them are walking past quite swiftly, with purpose, others roam around in huddles, arms linked, leaning back and laughing, joking, eating bread rolls out of peeled-back cloth napkins. They might only be fifteen, but they are called 'young women'. At fifteen you can sign a work contract, even I know that. But I, I couldn't sign a thing.

Some groups of women speak Kreol or Bhojpuri, loud and raucous, skirts swishing, and wide coloured collars nestling in their necks, with shawls and without shawls. Others speak strange languages from faraway places, just as loud and raucous, their clothes in unmatching mixtures. An evening skirt with a beach shoe. A girl's blouse with an old lady's trousers. I find myself looking for the girl from Kandos. Stupid. As if she could be here.

It must be that break time between the day's work and when the overtime starts at the free zone factories. Which reminds me it's a weekday. Yes, a Tuesday I think it is. I'd fallen into thinking it was Sunday. This morning seems days ago, weeks ago, months ago. Lifetimes ago.

Which means I'm losing touch now.

I have even forgotten I hate cars. I've forgotten about blades, the snake of rope, an old oil bottle of kerosene and a plastic bag of powder that's far too white. I have forgotten I failed HSC, forgotten I ever sat for that fucking exam.

I have also, all over again, completely forgotten there's an errand in my pocket.

Now I've gone and forgotten it's a weekday. Soon I'll forget they call me 'Boy'.

Suddenly, I realize I can hear the sound of a rapidly slowing-down car. Of sorts. This car, its every aspect, should have caused me to hesitate. I should have said to myself, 'Don't do it! Don't get into this broken-down cart, Krish!'

But I don't. Instead I say: 'Go for it! Why do you *hesitate* like that? Put your foot down, Krish! Accelerate into your new life.'

Too late in any case. My right arm is still up in the air, hand folded into a fist, thumb sticking out upwards, still actually wagging. I can't pretend it isn't. So, it's all over. The signal is loud and clear, even internationally recognized. It means only one thing: you are asking for a lift. If someone stops, they are accepting, and you have nothing else to do but get in, that's what it means. I asked for it. This car is saying 'yes, you got it'. Therefore it's a deal. Contract made. Signed and sealed.

I can sign a contract, I realize in fear. I have signed one.

An old Mini Traveller it is, maroon in colour. Missing the ground under it by a matter of inches.

Like the ones all shopkeepers used to ply to and fro to Porlwi in when I was in primary school, to go and fetch their tinned tuna tied up in piles of a dozen, long bars of soap in cardboard boxes, plastic bags of steel wool tied together like candyfloss, bundles of dried Bombay duck imported from India tied together in piles with a diameter of a foot, packets of mosquito coils. When I was a kid that is, before they started getting four-wheel drives and before the importers started delivering all this stuff to the shops in vans with signs on them saying 'THE DRIVER DOES NOT HAVE THE KEYS TO THE SAFE OF THIS VAN' so as to try to pre-empt hold-ups, which are rife. Two doors they had, those Mini Travellers, so the shopkeeper would lean the front passenger seat forwards to let a back passenger in – the whole seat would tip forwards – and then right at the back there was another door, a double door to open the boot, like a mini station wagon, for putting all the goods in. That kind of car.

Now one in front of me, a hand-painted maroon one, is scree-screeching to a halt. It swerves, jolts, and then after a second or two of motionlessness, its engine cuts out, right there in front of me. As if to announce: 'Here I am, then. Like it or not!'

I should have had the presence of mind to say I had changed my mind. I should have said I wanted to go north but had inadvertently stood on the wrong side of the road by mistake. *Error.* I should have said anything to get out of this.

But I just stood there. Waiting. Looking at the old Mini Traveller. Maroon in colour. Number L 404. *La 404.*

Just to look at it, I should have known what would be in store for me. How could you expect anything *ordinary* from such a car?

But I'm not sharp enough. Not on my toes enough. I'm slow on the uptake.

'Where exactly are you headed, mate?' A voice calls out from the passenger seat at me. He calls me 'mate'. That's better, anyway. On the other hand, when I look at that car, at its pitiful state, I, the son of a taxi driver, I say to myself, 'So what if he calls me mate'.

'Where you going then, sir?' I say, trapped by my own fear of having been born with bad manners. Not to be a 'breech' again.

'Just listen to this one! You sure hear strange things! Asks us where *we* are going! He's hitching, and he asks us our business. Well, truth is, mister, we don't know where we are going.' He looks at the driver, who starts to laugh loudly. Then he, the driver, says, 'Wherever you want to go. You just name the place, I'll take you there. That's all you have to do. Name it. Go on, name it. Beat that for a deal! Better than that you won't get anywhere, not in this damn world, anyway.'

Now I'm stuck. And I can't handle it.

'I-I-I don't know wh-where I'm going either,' I say, confused. I'm always getting confused. 'But you-you're heading for the north, aren't you?' Maybe I can wiggle out of it this way.

'Well, get in then anyway,' the driver replies, 'and we'll work it all out together.'

His passenger, thin and compact, jumps out, full of energy and style, and tilts his seat forwards graciously so as to let me in. A butler in a film. The driver, meanwhile, turns the ignition key. I see his hand on the steering wheel. It is huge. The size of four of my hands. I hear the dull attempt of the battery to turn the engine. *Nyuk*! No luck.

'No hurry to take any decisions, young man, democracy will rule! Climb in meanwhile,' he adds, 'and we'll see if she starts! Be a good girl, will you?' I can't take my eyes off the size of those hands on the steering wheel.

As I lean over to climb through the front door and into the back seat, I see, to my horror, that on the back of the back seat, just where I'm heading, there are the enormous heads of two large dogs, leaning over eagerly from the boot compartment into where I have to sit. White long-haired dogs with brown spots. There they are sitting, lurching into the space I've got to get into, pink tongues hanging out. We never had dogs at home. They are just where my head will be when I'll be sitting, where I'm *supposed* to sit. They're staring at me, all curiosity. They want to know who they've got for company. Their tongues loll this way and that. Their ears point forwards. Their noses work away, twitching round and round to try to find out by smell who I might be.

'Take no notice of them, in you get!' the driver says, 'Just give their heads a gentle shove. They'll move back, or over. But first, we all wish you welcome on board. I, your Captain, speaking on behalf of us all, wish you a good trip. I personally hope you enjoy your journey with us. And here is my assistant, "Kid" to his friends. A co-pilot, you could call him. Pleased to meet you.'

I don't manage a reply.

I am scared of dogs. I don't even manage to introduce myself. I'm not very good at these formal manners, anyway. I don't say anything at all. Nothing. I just stare back at the two dogs. They terrify me. They know I'm scared, too, and are taking advantage of it. I think I'll tell the driver it's OK, drive on without me.

'Get the hell out of there!' Captain bellows.

I think he is shouting at me, I cringe, but no, it's at the two dogs. He turns around in his seat, leans way over, grabs each by a muzzle, and forces their heads into the back corner behind him. Their bodies follow.

'Bloody bandit dogs!' he calls them, now rubbing roughly and affectionately a spot behind the bigger one's ears. 'The big one's a male, this one, Major. A fine dog. And that's his sweet, demented one-and-only daughter, the damsel Chanchal. Say how d'you do, dogs!'

'And my name's Krish,' I manage. Should I have given a false name? After lies, intention to impersonate. Too late anyway now.

'Pleased to meet you, Krish,' say Captain and Kid together. Like a song of some sort. Their names are like the title of a song: *Captain and the Kid*. The parents of Major and Chanchal. Adopting Krish. Some family.

'There we go,' Kid says, pulling me by my shoulder in after him, 'you take up a pew just there.' He dives into the back seat himself, cuddling the dogs' heads behind him, and gives up his place in the front for me. Yes, he lets me sit in the front seat.

I who have never experienced such selfless generosity.

Which means I am not in the back with the hounds of hell, but that I am nevertheless inside the car. Drawn in. *Bel e byen*. It is all over.

Captain tries to start up the car again. Nothing doing.

'Bad luck today. If it doesn't take on the third try, we've got no choice in the matter. Have to get out and push.' He tries a second time. No luck. A third time. Nothing.

'All passengers out and push!' He calls this out, as if he's got about twenty of us jammed in there. A whole crew.

So, I get out again. Maybe I'll manage to get away. Kid also gets out. And I start my ride by pushing the car instead. When you throw your lot in with people, that's it, it seems. There is no getting out of it again. There Kid and I are now, pushing, pushing, pushing, building up to a fine speed, almost running now. I whisper to myself, 'There you go, Krish! Shoulder to the wheel!' The wind in my ears, it's exciting. Captain puts the car into gear at just the exact right moment, it shakes, shudders, coughs, splutters, and then *takes*, letting out a glorious roaring sound. The car engine starts ticking over, music to our ears. And I, the new passenger, have changed already. Transformed. I'm in there, helter skelter. Kid and I have to run charging after the car to catch up.

Kid squirms through into the back seat once again, right in front of the two huge dogs, who, thrilled at all these events, now take to licking his ears, making him go ticklish. I climb into the front passenger seat once again. Close the door behind me.

'Fasten your seat belts, gentlemen,' Captain says. 'We have lift-off.'

'And you thought this was just an aeroplane, Krish,' I say to myself.

*

No sooner have we set off, happily hurtling along, the car rattling around us in light percussion with only an occasional heavy bass knock that could be worrying, than it begins to rain, but just the odd one big loud raindrop. A higher pitch. The rounded sounds of the woodwinds coming in. Plop, plop-plop, plop. I hadn't even noticed clouds forming. But now when I look up, I can see that there is just one big black cloud right up above us, in an otherwise clear blue sky. Is this a sign from above? Each drop of rain falls huge and loud, and then there are more and more, until they build up to a crescendo, blending in with the rattling, accompanied by the roar of the engine. It is the kind of rain that hurts when it falls on you. It is falling on my left arm. The smell of dust getting wet rises up out of the ground. And wet plants. I study the window arrangement, a two-piece sliding thing, but my window is jammed open forever. It doesn't close.

'Don't worry,' says Captain, 'mine doesn't close either.' The logic of the man is perfect.

By now I can't think. I don't know what to feel. It's like

I've hit a storyline. My life just starts to skid along in it. Happily. Could I lean back into it now? This music? It fills me with happiness. I can't even think any more.

Captain turns on the windscreen wipers, which come in now, quite high-pitched string instruments. He begins to sing. A tenor from some modern song, probably made up by him, himself.

'I'm beginning to enjoy this,' I mumble to myself. 'Oh, my god. I'm letting myself go.'

But I still keep my eyes on the road. My denim bag still sits tense on my knees, which are pressed tight together.

I'm suddenly scared now. My feelings zigzagging danger-ously. 'What kind of people are these? Where am I going? Why did I hitch a lift with them? They've even stopped talking about where we're going. Just singing now.' These are the thoughts that accompany my rising panic.

'Sling your bag into the back,' Captain says. Will Kid try to rob me? Both dogs are very pleased, and lean over and smell it impolitely. Probably still smells of the curried chicken innards and chilli cakes with holes in the middle. And vanilla. Kid starts to talk to the dogs now, yes, as if they are people. 'Don't be so nosy. Else your muzzles will get long. Then what!' We drive on, and on, and on. I begin to relax again. I am lulled into becoming one with the symphony. Rain cutting us off from everything else in the world. In a perfect cocoon. No talk. Just the roaring crescendo of the raindrops on the metalwork getting louder relative to all the other sounds. A sort of peace comes over me, then. They don't say anything for ages.

And I fall, as usual, into dreaming away. I see myself under a waterfall, naked, the water pounding on my back and shoulders. Now I am eating candyfloss at midnight on a deserted beach in the pouring rain, the sweet stuff all over my mouth, and on the other side of the candyfloss is the girl from Kandos, her hair lifting and showing a neck so perfectly poised. Then there's Baya and me, we're running, running, running after a rabbit in thick cane fields in the pouring rain, both wearing the same pair of running shoes. Then I see Kid, he's standing on top of the mountain at Mamu Dip's lecturing to a whole team of dogs of different shapes and sizes, all with their tongues lolling out crookedly, all taking notes studiously. In the pouring rain.

Only to find that I snap back to thinking whether I'll have to try and escape.

As if I were a prisoner.

'Oh, damn it! The bonnet!' Captain says. I haven't been listening really, so I don't click what he says. But I don't let on either. He pulls up the car on the side of the road, and stops without turning the engine off. On the contrary, he is revving like mad.

'Just give it a push,' he says to me, 'Get out, go round, and give it a push. It's easy. I don't want to get out in case she cuts out again.'

I have been so deep in my dreams, so far away watching Kid speaking to all those dogs like that and then wondering if I will get a chance to run for it, that I just look at Captain blankly. I see that he is pointing at the front of the car in that pouring rain. So, I just obey. As if it's a conditioned reflex. *Obey.* I open the door, get out, run to the front of the car in that downpour, drenched I am, already in those few seconds. Then I realize I don't have the foggiest idea what I am supposed to do. So I stand there and signal with my hands: *What am I supposed to do?* Turning my palms upwards.

He is signalling madly from inside. Now, pointing

outside the window, round towards the bonnet. But the only things I can see, and they attract my attention because they are moving, are the two windscreen wipers batting away rhythmically. Does he want me to stop them? I decide to try to catch them. When I try to grab them here, they turn round and go there. When I try to grab them there, they come back here. Stupid things!

I see Captain, darting like an arrow out of the car, shouting at me, 'What the hell do you think you're doing, wooden-handed idiot? Uproot my fucking windscreen wipers? Clown!' He pushes me aside, and leans heavily on both his hands on the bonnet and clicks it down into place. I now see just how huge Captain's frame is. It's not just his hands. He is a giant. I feel shrunken.

'Oh, so that's what I was supposed to do, Mr Captain,' I confess.

'I am not *Mr* Captain to you either. Captain, that's all. Where were you then? Dreamland? Head in the clouds?'

The engine has cut out again.

My fault now.

Kid has also got out by now, and is in the pelting rain, all taut and wound up, ready for pushing. He is laughing. So we all laugh together. And I relax now, more thoroughly. We just stand there in the pouring rain and laugh. I who've never known anything like this.

Captain gets back in. Kid isn't even cross with me. He doesn't mind getting wet. We just start pushing the car, he and I, until it takes. Easy does it. Then Kid says, 'Rather you get in the back, you, you're useless as far as cars go, that's for fucking sure. Don't want to piss Captain off with your idiocy.' They wouldn't believe it if I said my father's got a taxi. Lucky they don't know.

I lean in, brace myself for it, and go through to the back

seat. The two big dogs, Major and Chanchal, at once set about smelling my ears, loudly. Cold noses on my hot ears. I freeze. They smell of wet dog. The bit of car above them leaks copiously.

'Gotcha!' Captain says, 'Found you out. You don't wash your ears!' Then he adds, just when you think he might be being nasty, 'Just their way of saying they love you. They *do* like you, Krish, can't you tell? Look at their tails. Feel their cold noses. Isn't it the happiest feeling?'

No, I think to myself, it isn't.

Captain leans over to Kid, and I think I catch what he says: '*Piti la enpe abriti, non?*' He thinks I'm screwed up.

We set off again. Yes, their long, fluffy white tails are wagging. They are not very fluffy dogs, but they've got fluffy tails. Wagging, round and round.

'We also like you,' he adds, addressing me in the rear-view mirror. He and Kid both laugh out loud. As though it's true, as though they do like me. Captain will drive me wherever I want to go, and Kid has already offered me his place once.

Or should I be dead scared of these two? Maybe I should be. Or not. They seem to be fond of one another in a way. Gentle. Tender. Almost love between them, you could say, but not really. On good terms with one another, anyway. At ease. Not a bad vibration between them.

He doesn't stay mad at me, that's for sure, Captain doesn't. He just takes up a song again: '*Singin' in the rain.*' When you think of it, I nearly tore out his windscreen wipers, and all he does is sing.

*

While we are driving along, the two dogs, as if they have decided it as a plot, begin to insinuate themselves from the back compartment on to the seat next to me. One to the right of me, and one to the left. I am in a vice.

'Clever Alecs,' Kid congratulates them. The dogs are both pleased. Thrilled they are, having got out of the rainy boot. I am still terrified of them. So, they decide to put me at ease, and gradually each one rolls itself into a well-calculated circle, meaning both their heads are resting on my lap. A picture we are. Me in the middle, Major on my right, and his daughter, Chanchal, on my left. They immediately fall fast asleep. At least I think they do. Although I must admit I can hear a sort of teeth-grinding sound. Maybe that's what dogs do when they are asleep? Maybe they are wide awake and up to something? So, I pluck up the courage to lean over and look at them, trying not to disturb them. Their eyes are closed. All is well. And I am too scared to move any more than this. So I just sit still, a sphinx, between the two hellhounds.

At least they keep me warm as I dry out.

As we get to the Pamplemus Gardens, the rain stops as suddenly as it started, and the sky above all that lush green is blue. We see all the magnificent trees, trees that make people look so tiny underneath them, *put us in our place*, trees all washed down, fresh, each one a grand and beautiful witness, a silver-trunked, wide-branched, million-leafed marvel, reaching from deep under the ground high up into the sky. But then, in a moment, those same trees seem to change. They begin to look eerie to me. Maybe they really are spirits with their heads buried under the ground, and their bodies, legs and arms doomed to flail around perpetually in the sky making desperate patterns to express their suffering. Never in all my life have I seen the Gardens this way. To me they are usually just there. Ordinary. A fuss about nothing. But today, they send out sparkling rays of perfection one minute and then eerie mysterious meanings the next.

Captain says: 'Look at the different colours of green – you could swim in them! Leafy speafy!' and Kid replies, 'Look at the height of that one. It's touching the sky. And o-o-oh! The rainbow. It starts in that tree's leaves and it arches across the whole sky, look, to where the gold is. We are blessed, Captain and Krish. We are blessed, Major and Chanchal. Please can we stop, Captain. Can we buy a lottery ticket, Captain?'

'You know, Krish,' Captain ignores Kid, 'sometimes we go and pick up cashew nuts from under the giant cashew nut tree in the middle of the Garden. But don't tell anyone. We don't want every Tom, Dick and Harry knowing about collecting cashew nuts, do we? A little knowledge is a dangerous thing,' at which Kid laughs. 'Like to come with us one day, Krish?'

I'm so honoured, I can't even answer at first. I just mumble: 'Love to.'

I see the Captain, in just one look, signalling the Kid that he was right, I am a bit screwed up. Let me be.

But there's no time for me to dwell on that look. We are moving on.

In a matter of minutes we are heading for the motorway, and we find ourselves right on one of its feeder roads. All signposted with white arrows on blue, and everything. At this moment, we suddenly hear the alarming sound of an over-revved accelerator, and the car jerks forward. Enough to break our necks. Captain forces the gears into neutral like an ace, and this slows the car at once, while the sound goes on, hectic with revs.

'Jammed accelerator,' Captain announces, adding swearwords liberally. He brakes now, and the car comes to a halt.

He turns off the ignition. 'This car belongs to the Diocese, you know,' he says.

You never know what he will come out with next.

'Diocese? What d'you mean Diocese?'

'Well, I mean the Diocese of Porlwi, of course. What other Diocese is there? The Anglican one?'

I can't believe it. I begin to think they are spinning me all kinds of stories just so they can see how truly gullible I am. Or for the sheer pleasure of their own confabulation. But then again, their reality is not unlike a dream. Two men and their dogs in an old Mini Traveller, broken down on the feeder road on to the motorway. And talking about the Diocese, whose property they say the car is. 'It belonged to a priest who went abroad. He gave it to us, before he left. He liked us. At the time, anyway. Just like we picked you up at the junction there, because we like you.'

These guys will say anything.

'You stay in the car, Major and Chanchal and Krish. Meanwhile, we will see to this little cable problem. The limousine will be back to normal in no time.' So I'm classified with the dogs now. *Sit, Boy!*

'OK,' I say.

No doubt a stolen car. That's what I think. Couldn't they have stolen something better, though? Something more reliable? I mean while they were about it. Listen to what I'm saying now. I who am already going about in stolen cars, for that matter. Stolen goods. Receiving the benefits of stolen goods. After swearing and lying, now I'm receiving stolen goods. What would my mother say?

The big dog, Major, goes on grinding away at his teeth.

The other one, Chanchal, puts her head sweetly on my shoulder now, like we're two lovers on the back seat of the car. I am sorely tempted to feel content. I am sorely tempted to stop worrying about everything.

At this very moment, I whisper to myself: 'Lucky you, then. Maybe you should just learn to purr now, Krish.'

And so it came about that they fixed the accelerator cable in no time, and were back in the car, raring to go.

It is only now that I look down at my T-shirt. Major has bitten a huge hole in the front of it. That's what he was doing with the teeth grinding. Captain and Kid think it's the funniest thing they ever saw, and they double up with laughter, until they cry and their tummies hurt. They are not in the least responsible, nor do they care. 'Keep your eye on the road,' I think, but all I say is, 'Never mind, I've got a spare.'

'So, you stayed overnight somewhere, then?' says Kid.

'Yeah. Stayed with the Uncle and Aunt a couple of days.'

Now, I begin to tell lies *for nothing*. And with the greatest of ease. Why couldn't I have said I was *going* to stay with them, but didn't? What would it have cost me to tell them the truth? Or am I scared of telling the truth now? Is the truth too complicated for me now?

'We're getting on to the motorway now. So, it's decision-making time. Northwards? Or is it down to the west coast, then? Speak up!'

He starts going round the roundabout in the limousine. He has settled his steering wheel on perpetual circles. Round and round we go. He loves it. Kid loves it too. I never did anything like this in my father's taxi, I can tell you.

'West?' Kid asks, indifferent really.

64

'Your opinion on this, Krish?' He is still going round and round the roundabout, again and again, making a merry-go-round out of a roundabout, that's what he can do, Captain.

'Agreed!' I say, hoping not to get dizzy.

'The precise destination to be determined at a later date, all in good time,' Captain adds.

So we set off again, in a straightish line, for down the west coast.

They laugh and joke and mess about until I join in at some point, and begin to laugh along with them.

Exams have left me altogether. Results have moved even further away from me. Gone into thin air. Volatilized. Disappeared. Instead of making myself disappear, I've made *those things* disappear. Who would have thought that was possible?

Suddenly, as we are picking up speed, going full tilt along the motorway, not yet having decided what our exact destination is but nevertheless speeding towards it, Captain and Kid singing with their heads thrown back, when we are somewhere around the Rosbwa roundabout in the middle of all the late afternoon traffic coming the other way, we hear a kind of explosion which throws the limousine off balance, out of control, makes it skid then spin around full circle, until Captain gains control again, and slows it down, tames it altogether, and then brings it to a halt on the shoulder of the motorway.

'Events, events, events!' Captain exclaims.

All three of us get out, me folding my T-shirt over so that the hole doesn't show, and we close the two doors behind us so the dogs don't get out on to the motorway. That would spell disaster, Kid says.

'A tyre must have exploded,' I say.

'Oh, didn't know we had a resident diagnostician with us,' Captain says to Kid, all admiration.

Kid gets out the spare and the tools, jacks the car up, changes the tyre. All goes well. To him this is nothing at all. No problem.

'He could work for Schumacher,' I say.

'He already does,' Captain replies, tall, and taking a bow.

'Let's go to Kan Yolof, get this fixed,' Captain says. 'No need to tempt fate by driving around without a spare. Teasing and insulting gods, that would be. What you say, Kid?'

Which is what we do. And soon, our Mini Traveller slips off the motorway and into the mixture of new square blocks of flats, jammed against old wooden and tin houses so perfect they could be models, next to houses handmade out of cardboard and plastic sheeting, hiding between hardware godowns, and everywhere huge trees bulging out between stone walls. Just off the motorway.

There is a sign up in three versions: 'Isi nu kol fit', 'Vulcanization', 'Your tyres repaired'. Not that you needed a sign. The three eight-year-olds who man the place are already sinking the inner tubing of the burst tyre into a big once-white bathtub full of filthy grey water, so they can locate the puncture. Then they stick a matchstick in the hole, and prepare the hot irons for doing the vulcanization. They pump the tyre up again afterwards with a hand pump, judging the amount of pressure by relying on their own experience on the job.

'Could you workers please put the old tyre back in its original place at the back here, and put this spare back in the boot,' Captain says, giving orders to the eight-year-olds. 'That spare is too smooth and shiny, even for our taste.'

'Goes well, this old pile of iron?' one of the child repairers ventures, getting ready to run in case he's made this big man cross.

'This, my son,' Captain replies, 'is a *limousine*. Never lets us down.'

Bit of a lie, I think to myself, given that we have just had to push, and that we broke down a few minutes earlier and had to stop and repair the accelerator cable.

'Give the dogs some water in that hubcap, Krish,' Captain says.

I am pleased that I have earned an order to do something. And of course I don't fail to notice that Captain is getting the dogs to take water from *me*, so that I gain some confidence in myself.

Holding on to my T-shirt front to hide the hole, I go and fetch some water from the tap by the bathtub. I pass Major and Chanchal the full hubcap. They drink loudly and messily and with great gusto.

'Must remember to take them for a pee later,' Captain says. 'This is the first time we have brought these two vagabonds along with us on an outing.' I'd thought they had been doing it for centuries.

We set off again.

'We've got to decide where we are actually going now. It's nearly five o'clock,' Captain says.

I've meanwhile lost all notion of time. I haven't got any bearings left. I can only remember the lie I told Uncle Dip about having to leave at four o'clock. Just one hour ago?

'Let's go to Flikanflak. The beach at Flikanflak. The public beach. The dogs will have space there, and we can snorkel around a bit before the sun goes down,' Kid suggests. I now know why there are two pairs of flippers, two snorkels and two pairs of goggles in a plastic bag where the dogs are supposed to sit. The plastic bag is next to a case of beer with two flimsy dog chains draped over it.

'What's your view, Krish? You agree with that plan?'

'Agree. Hundred per cent.'

Then I muster up some sense, and ask, 'Where will you be going after that?' I become responsible for one minute.

'I'll go up towards Kat Born perhaps,' Captain says vaguely, 'No need to worry about a thing.' And then, as an afterthought, he adds: 'How old are you, by the way?'

Captain is no fool.

While he is driving, his mind is working at the same time. Unlike mine, which has stopped working entirely.

I really have to think fast now though.

'Who, me? Why, eighteen,' I reply, immediately regretting having said the 'Who, me' first. Makes my age sound made up. And the 'Why' makes me sound like a liar, too. I even detect a giveaway lift in intonation in the 'eighteen', as if it needed a question mark.

So, this is my first real *lie* lie. My first fully-fledged, adult, unadulterated and with criminal intent to mislead, lie.

Not just an honest-to-goodness lie, but a serious one. A lie that can change all sorts of things. A lie with legal effect. A proper lie. With consequences. On Captain. On Kid. And on me.

'You sure?' Captain checks.

'Yes, sir,' I answer. 'Sure as sure can be.' Again I regret my own words. Why did I go and add that 'as sure can be'? And the 'sir' sounded phony, even to me.

'I don't go for that "as can be", you know Krish, to be frank,' Captain says, genuinely concerned for the first time.

'I've just written my HSC,' I say, 'so I am eighteen.'

'Mmm,' is all Captain says.

We speed along, and in what seems like no time at all, fast forward, we are driving into Flikanflak. We go right past the fish-landing station, louts sitting around telling jokes in the shade of the open kiosk, through the village bustling with afternoon things, past the police station and the coast guard, and into the middle of a patch of young casuarina trees, the sky above suddenly thick with grey-green needles, clustered like millions of stars, and magic shiny tiny tight hard green cones like thousands of elliptical planets, right at the beginning of the public beach.

Captain turns the car around to face the way back, before coming to a stop, I suppose so that, if we need to push when we set off again later, we can get the advantage of a straight line and some slightly downward-sloping hard sand in front of the car.

I am learning now.

'Just in case,' he says. As if there were some infinitesimally small risk involved.

'You stay with the limousine, Krish, and keep an eye on the dogs, will you? You can let them wander about. They'll come back all by themselves when they are ready to, don't worry. And don't get into trouble looking at girls' legs on the beach while we're gone, mind.' I look down, like he found me out.

And how can he be so sure about the dogs coming back? He only just told me it was the first time they were bringing these vagabond dogs on an outing. But I don't say anything.

I've been given a third task. After the bonnet and the dogs' water.

'Kid and I are nipping out for a quick dive. Just to the reef and back.' *Nipping out*. I look up. *Quick dive*. It is at least half a mile to the reef there. They strip to their underpants, get their snorkelling equipment out, spit on the inside of their goggles and start rubbing methodically and then dipping them in the seawater. They hide two illegal underwater arrows in their underpants and along the line of their thighs, and they're off.

They abandon me all on my own with that clapped-out limousine and those two lousy hounds.

The first thing I do is take off my wet T-shirt with the huge wet hole in the middle of it, swear at the dogs, pull my spare T-shirt out of my denim bag, and put it on. Nice and dry. Then, I take a long, hard look at my ruined T-shirt, imagining what my mother will make of it, and what I will say when she asks. No good will come of it, I think. So, I kneel down and dig a hole with my bare hands in the sand. Only when I have reached a full arm's length do I bury the whole thing.

'Well done,' I whisper to myself, 'Destroy all suspicious clues.'

Covering up the signs. I'm becoming a habitual criminal. A recidivist. A repeater. The word brings me up sharp. The 'repeaters' class. I won't go back to that. Upper Sixth repeaters. Habituals. I won't re-go to school, re-suffer, or re-fail. No. Never.

'Haven't left home a day, and I'm burying my clothing in strange places,' I muse.

I suddenly remember my errand. I press my hand against my trouser pocket. The errand is still there. Nicely in its place.

I stare out now at the sea, watching my two new friends as they walk out along a sandbank. Are they *friends* to me? The word doesn't make me go to pieces any more anyway. But I get this fleeting thought: *If only Baya was here now.*

Then Major and Chanchal come into my line of sight. They begin by following Captain and Kid into the sea for a while, then lose interest in this game. They don't want to get their stomachs and chests wet. Paws and legs is one thing.

So, what do they decide to do instead? They decide to start drinking the seawater. First hesitantly, and then with relish. I rush up to try and dissuade them. How do you dissuade dogs from drinking seawater? Beg? Shout? Hit?

They go on drinking it. Like it's milky tea.

What can I do? I plead. But it doesn't work.

I decide to ignore them instead.

I go and sit down and stare at the sea.

I concentrate on the beauty of it. *Or try to.* Or the poetry of it. Here I am sitting on the golden-silver sand of the beach, casuarina trees murmuring behind me, the reef rumbling to comfort me in the distance, a lagoon turning from turquoise to orange as I look out at what promises to be a magnificent sunset, asking myself how far I am seeing when I look out to sea. Five miles? And then where is the nearest anything other than sea? Is it Madagascar? A thousand miles away. More. A word comes into my head now, from the thought of that distance. *Free.* I breathe free air. Me and the big sun, silly me and the big sun. Is it about to lean down and kiss the sea in a ritual of fire meeting water? Will there be a loud hissing noise? Or, if I look down to my left, would I, if I went straight, get to the South Pole?

Exam results begin to stray and to get further and further away from my mind now. Further than the South Pole. Further than the sun. I see a child's kite is now dancing in front of the sun, trying to attract the sun's attention, teasing it.

I'm relieved to see the dogs have stopped drinking seawater. It must be me ignoring them, and thinking about beauty and nature and poetry.

They have decided to hunt crabs instead.

Nothing wrong with that.

But, oh no, that's not all they are doing. Now they are digging right next to a tourist lady. She is still sunbathing, with some glistening special oil on her back, although the sun has just about disappeared, and they have turned their backs to her and are beginning to dig a huge hole right next to her. They are hurling sand from between their legs, directly on top of her. By the pad-full. I pretend I don't know the dogs. They aren't mine after all. Not even a lie this time.

No, I feel too sorry for her now. Don't know what cold miserable country she's come from for a bit of setting sun, don't know how much money she's gone and saved up and paid some travel agent to get to this dumb bit of beach. She shouldn't have to go through this now.

So I start calling them: 'Major, good dog, Chanchal, my puppy,' and so on.

To no effect. They go on digging and digging. With abandon now. As though I'm encouraging them. Like cartoon dogs. Dig-dig-digging. Sending more and more sand up into the sky and down on to the lady. She is furious.

I try yelling at them. Loudly and harshly, I cry, 'Come here, you filthy mongrels!'

I get up now, and hurry over to the scene of the incident, and try to intervene physically. I grab Major's front legs.

This earns me a mouthful of swearing from the English lady, 'Can't you control your pets? For god's sake.' But then she notices that I'm scared of the dogs, so she laughs at me. The dogs meanwhile think it's all a game, and Major starts biting on my new shirt.

'I'm sorry. They're not mine. They're my friends'. And my friends are in the sea, swimming off.'

'Into the bloody sunset,' she says, and turning her back on me and the two dogs, she gets up with a sigh, picking up her towel and oil, and moves further along the beach, maybe back to her hotel. Her back is covered in a layer of sand, stuck to the oil.

Thank god they don't follow her. They persist with the crab-hunting instead. Loyal to it. Probably an imaginary crab, knowing these two.

Now what! Major and Chanchal are off at a literal gallop. High speed, with their tails out straight behind them. Never seen dogs' tails like that. Out and across the main road, with car brakes screeching around them, over to the cemetery on the other side.

Strings of cars in both directions, driving too fast.

I panic. What if they get run over? Captain put me in charge. Keep an eye on them, he said.

So, I run after them. But at the same time, I have to keep looking back to keep an eye on the car as well. What if someone steals it?

Not that I can, in all frankness, imagine a car thief so low as to steal that limousine. I wouldn't take it for free. No one in their right mind would. Other than those two. Not that I'm sure about their minds.

I stand on this side of the main road and watch the dogs. Now what! Look at them! They've gone and got diarrhoea. Must be all that seawater they've drunk. That fast? I'm shocked. It's gone right through them. Squirting out.

The real runs, and under pressure. They curl their

♦

73

bottoms right under, and are forcing away, and the crap is coming out in jets.

Ah, relief. They're coming back again now. They manage to get across the road without getting run over. Thank goodness for that.

But it's not over. They are thirsty now, after all that salt water, and after all the runs. It's normal, they are desperately thirsty. So what do they do? They go down to the sea again, and go right into the water, and I can't stop them, they start drinking seawater all over again.

Again, in no time, they are charging across the main road. More runs. Then they are coming back again. Get thirsty, drink more water.

I give up.

I sit down and I take the formal decision not to worry about something I can't change. I can't change them drinking salt water, charging across the road, getting runs, coming back again, getting thirsty, etc. It's just one of the many things in this world that I can't do anything about.

It's not even a question of pretending that they aren't my dogs. Because they are not my dogs. It's a fact. I feel myself beginning to get confused. I couldn't give a damn, I try to think. If they die under a car, it's not my fault. And nastily I think, they are only dogs, anyway.

But now they decide to break their routine. They have seen something interesting. Something *new*. A horse. A retired racehorse that is being led by a frail little old man who is taking a tiny child for a gentle ride. A *small business*, they call it, this type of enterprise. Take a retired racehorse, get children to get on it one by one, lead the horse about on the beach for a while, pose for a photograph and then take some rupees off the parent. Creates employment, the government says on the TV. Rather a horse than a car any day, I think to myself. It's cute.

Major and Chanchal also think it's cute. Or they haven't ever seen a horse before. Or they know how to cause me problems. I don't know which. But they decide to annoy the horse. To run after the horse, yes, to chase the thing around the beach. With a child on it. Trying to get at the horse's shins. The man leading the horse starts to get angry, quite rightly so, I think, and is shooing them away. But they are persistent. They want to tease that horse, annoy the hell out of it.

This I cannot ignore.

What if the horse panics? What if it bucks the child off? This is serious. I will be in the wrong. Rightly so. These dogs are a public nuisance now. A danger. At large. And I am in charge. I was formally put in charge of them. *Keep an eye on the dogs, will you, Krish?*

I rush up to the big father dog, Major, take all my courage and grab him by the extra skin around his neck, and pull really hard, a body tackle. He is heavy, but he buckles. I think I must have hurt him. And once I get Major out of the game, Chanchal follows. There's another bit of learning: Chanchal follows Major.

So, they go and drink seawater again.

I'm getting fed up now. Why don't I just get on a bus and get out of here.

But then again, I can't just leave like that. I am in charge of the car. A limousine. I'm in charge of the dogs. Major and Chanchal.

And what if the dogs follow me to the bus stop and right on to the bus? So I go and stand on the edge of the sea and start yelling: 'Captain, Kid!' But their two pairs of flippers just go on flap-flapping, flap-flapping, rhythmically against the cool surface of the afternoon lagoon, making white splashes on the blue around them. On and on. Oblivious. I scream: 'Captain! Kid!' But they can't hear a thing. Their snorkels move further and further out. As if they've got a meeting fixed with the sun for when it kisses the water. Flap-flapping flippers.

'Captain! Help! Come back! Kid! Can't you hear me?'

When I'm standing there in despair, Major, I can't say why, just comes right up to me and does something to *try* me. Maybe he was scared in case he lost his bearings, maybe he thought he might lose Captain and Kid – lost at sea like sailors – and might need to fall back on me. Maybe he wasn't sure he would recognize me instantly. Anyway, he just swaggers over to me, lifts his hind leg, and pees on my trouser leg.

'Filthy hound! First you bite a hole in my T-shirt, then you piss on my jeans,' I scream. But what's the point in getting cross with an animal? He won't understand. Maybe his intention was a good one, who knows. Maybe it's the only present he knows how to give.

No, the fact is there. I am being pissed on. By male dogs.

I sit down to take off Baya's running shoes and my socks, almost crying now, and then I wade into the sea to wash my jeans clean. I am falling in the world now, I have become a lamppost for male dogs, I have become an inanimate object.

At long last Captain and Kid come back. Bearing with them a nice medium-sized octopus.

They laugh as though I'm telling stand-up comedy when I recount it all. They even say, 'Quite a storyteller, then. Does it run in the family?'

Have I walked into the vacuum Baya left? He, the storyteller, left an empty space, and I have been sucked into it. The dogs lap water from Kid's goggles.

I think of Renuka Mami, too. Would *she* like these two? For them, life is just a series of stories, one after the other, stories that they are living as they happen. And I have just chanced to fall into one of them. Or *some* of them. They are a peripatetic circus, and when it was going by, I just walked in by mistake and became part of it and its stories.

Strangely, they bring order with them.

'*Juri,*' Captain says. They at once put me in charge of the tinder while they go and collect the real wood. The dogs are immediately interested in our plans, as if they moved in with humans long ago, a million years ago. Which maybe they did. And maybe they know what will happen next. Then I begin to glow inside. All five of us, as we sit, three humans and two dogs, trying to get a fire to take, I feel the happiest I've ever felt in my whole life.

We watch the sun pout its lips as it kisses the pouting sea. I can't help it. I think of her, the girl at Kandos. Her eyes meeting mine. No clouds in just that bit of sky where the sun is going down. And everywhere there's helter-skelter colour, reds and oranges, pomegranate and vermilion, scarlet and crimson, blood-red, and firecracker red, maroon and mandarin, fire-red. In the sky and in the lagoon, everywhere red. And then when the colour suddenly starts to drain and then to fade into mauve and then grey, there is a hiatus, such a silence, and Captain says, 'Watch for something special now: a green flash, maybe.' And sure enough. The whole sky and the whole lagoon in unison pulse emerald green, turquoise green, leaf green. One long pulse. Like a hushed prayer. And then it is over.

'Peace,' Captain says, like a religious man. 'We have been shown the blue sea, red. And we have been shown the whole blue sky and the whole blue sea, green. Rare.'

'Content,' Kid replies, 'I am.'

'It's so calm here,' I say, 'Tranquil.'

No sooner has the word 'tranquil' been said, than we hear a kind of explosion.

'Bwf-bang!'

'Something has exploded!' I venture.

'The diagnostician strikes again,' Captain says, 'Need to sit for HSC exams to know that one.' I note that even in this time of crisis, he takes the trouble to be precise. He says 'sit for HSC' instead of 'have HSC'. They both, I realize, must know that I have *failed*. That I have recently found out that I have failed. That I wanted to die. That's how sensitive they are. That is why they are looking after me like this. Well, maybe. All this I know in the middle of this 'bang!'

'Look at the dogs,' I cry. 'Why are they barking at our car, then?' Note that I'm beginning to refer to this foul limousine as *our* car.

'Right you are,' Captain says.

'One of the tyres must have exploded,' Kid reckons.

'Yes, that must be it,' Captain replies.

Gingerly, we approach the car. As if there was a bomb in it. The dogs go on circling it, and barking at it, closing in on it. There is a kind of halo of dust around it, dust hovering and moving slightly up and out into the air. Together the three of us peer at the two left-side wheels. Our heads together, concentrating. They're OK. Fine. Then we walk around, still gingerly, like a bomb-disposal team, and look at the two right-side tyres, on the other side. Everything fine there, too. Intact. Whole. Nothing the matter with those two tyres either. So, we go back and look at the left-side ones again. It's got to be left or right.

But, no.

No, it doesn't. It's neither.

'But, it's just not possible,' Captain says.

The dogs go on barking at the car. The cloud of dust around the car begins to settle slowly. The limousine looks extra-terrestrial for a moment. With trepidation, we three go nearer and peep inside.

The spare tyre in the boot has exploded.

*

'Well, let's have a beer to celebrate.' We relax as Kid says this, 'Only a spare tyre.' Captain is cleaning the octopus on a rock with his pocket knife. I haven't even got a pocket knife, I muse to myself. He does this while the fire is taking, and then when it takes, he is ready to put the octopus on to grill, on the end of a wire fork he has just made.

'Later we'll drop you at Montan Bol, if that suits you. *When* we go up. *If.* Meanwhile, let's drink to our health. And to our friendship. That's what's important in life. *Friends.* Agree, Krish?'

He waits for an answer.

'Yeah, but the word *friend* haunts me sometimes.'

Captain frowns at this.

'Well, let's check then to see if drinking to friends is good, shall we? Test it in practice!'

So he gets out a can opener, and opens the three bottles of Phoenix Kid has brought out, one after the other in quick succession, hands them out, calling over a peanut vendor at the same time, and buying three packets of roasted peanuts with their skins dyed shocking pink.

Colour from the sky and lagoon, now concentrated in the peanut skins.

'Cheers!' they say to me. We hold up the three amber bottles to the fire.

'Cheers!' I reply. But of course it's a toast to much more than friendship.

And this is how I taste my first mouthful of alcohol. Bitter sweetness. What would my mother say? Is this worse than sausages? Or not so bad? I don't know.

'Eat up your peanuts fast,' Captain tells me. 'Or you'll get drunk on that empty stomach of yours.'

So, on a wide public beach, under a sky that changes colour like magic, I eat shocking pink peanuts and then grilled octopus.

And we drink to beauty now, beauty of the sky. Through the neck of an amber beer bottle.

'Sure you're eighteen?'

'Sure,' I nod. But my head is a little hesitant in the way it nods. 'Absolutely certain.' Again I choose my words badly.

*

When we are driving up the road from Flikanflak, we begin to notice a funny smell in the limousine. A burning smell. We all sniff loudly. Burning rubber. In a little downhill section in the mainly uphill road, Captain switches off the ignition and goes on sniffing as we free-wheel a few yards. He puts his head out of the window and sniffs again. The smell is just as bad when the engine's off.

So it's not the engine. I'm scared to say anything in case he calls me a 'diagnostician' again. He switches the engine on again, in case there's trouble restarting it, then he brakes, and brings the car to a halt. He leaves the engine ticking over on high revs.

Kid and I get out. We look at the wheels one by one, and find that there is a bit of car chassis scraping the left back wheel, causing the rubber to melt and smell burnt like that.

'Damn! No spare tyre left either,' I swear. 'Tempting gods, we were. You were right, Captain.'

'No problem,' Captain says, 'I'll go slowly. It's only rubbing slightly, isn't it? She'll take us home yet, that left rear tyre.' I realize that I don't even know where home is for them.

So we drive on, slow. Real slow.

Captain sings '*It's a long way to Tipperary*'. He's got songs for everything.

I say I'm not going to get off at Montan Bol. I will stay with them until Banbu just in case the car needs pushing.

'Thanks,' they say, 'most kind of you.'

As we are going into Banbu, just opposite the entrance to the Medinn sugar estate, where the white-barked trees on each side of the road are so huge that they meet in the middle, making a tunnel, we hear another explosion. Third in one day.

This time we all get out and tear around to the left rear tyre, which must have exploded.

But no, it hasn't.

Wrong again. There it is, still in fine shape. All plump and happy. Only slightly burnt in a line around its circumference.

'I don't believe it,' Captain says. 'Don't tell me.'

We walk around the car, all three of us together, to do an inspection.

Another tyre, the front right one, has exploded.

*

So we push the car to a mechanic called Jaynan's place. He's got a corrugated-iron workshop on the main road for fixing cars, motorbikes and bicycles. With all the spare parts anyone could ever need piled up high on top of the tin roof. Just opposite the Siwala. He says, no problem, he'll fix the two tyres in no time at all. He and his brother will.

So this is how we come to be standing like that, chatting on the edge of the road in Banbu in the dark. No problem.

*

I know I'll have to leave them here. Our paths will *part*. There'll be another *parting*. The words bring twinges to my chest. Paths diverging, theirs and mine. One this way, one that way. I feel moved, even troubled. I feel as though I'm having to *part* from people I've known all my life. Ridiculous. Or maybe, maybe they are my Baya in another form. Maybe he is in disguise as Captain-and-Kid and has come back to honour me with a visit from the other side. A brief reincarnation into two lives instead of just one. Now a new parting.

I reprimand myself now: 'Stop these thoughts! And your other delaying tactics. Get going, on your feet, now, walk! Lazybones! It's time to set off on your own now! Are you ready? On your marks, get set.'

I will have to start walking now. It's true. I'll have to go home to Karo Lalyann, and it'll have to be by foot. *But I don't want to go home to Karo Lalyann.* What if those results invade me again? I couldn't stand it. Being thrown away like that. I've got no defences. I've only just started clearing the results away, like so much debris, from my head. What if my mother invades me again? Not to mention my father ignoring me. I know they will for sure make me unhappy, and I don't want that either. I don't want them calling me 'Boy'. I couldn't stand it. Nor do I want to face that blade, nor that snake rope, powder that's too white, nor matches, either, because it'll only be another failure. Like the man halfway down the tree tops under the Montayn Ory Bridge.

I want to go *through* these partings instead, parting from these two, parting from my Baya. I don't want to skim over the top any more.

So, before I go home, I'll keep a bit more time for myself. Catch some time in my arms. Get a-hold of it. Feel it going through me, like I'll be going through it. A mutual thing. A time to *go through* saying goodbyes. Sounds stupid. But is that what it is? My time? I don't know.

But, eventually, in the end, I'll have to go back home, because I can't possibly spend the night out of doors. It's impossible.

These thoughts flit through my mind, staccato fashion.

And so it comes about that I do leave Captain and Kid. I manage to leave them. I tear myself away from them.

They are still there, chatting to Banbu people, deciding difficult things like whether or not to have another beer.

*

I go a short distance, 200 golet or so. I would usually call it 600 yards or 500 metres. But today, when I'm telling you, I know it's about 200 golet.

And here I am now, standing on the edge of the road, right in the middle of the village of Banbu, opposite the police station, looking at the Belil River going past on my left side. I stand watching it. It is there, and it is passing. Like time spent with Captain and Kid, it is moving, but still. Moving on, but calm. With *bred sonz* growing thick, heart-shaped, shiny, dark-green and edible on each heavily shaded bank.

'Salaam, my Captain. Salaam Kid.' That's how I say goodbye. Looking at the river instead of at them. The sadness stays with me. I walk on about fifty yards, then stop and watch the Belil River again, as it heads for the sea. Everything moves on. Everything passes. Everything changes. *Shanti shanti shanti*. But, when I'm with them, life is full of *happenings*. Every minute a new something happens. All by itself. *Happens* for the very first time in the history of the world. They just wait for it. And they've got another thing, they have. They've got *good faith*. Nothing else. Just a car and two dogs and good faith. Not that I even know what good faith is.

Until recently they didn't even have a car, I'm sure of that. I'm also sure they were happy when they didn't have

84

one. Now they've got their limousine. A terrible little vehicle. But there also, they are happy with it. Right now, they are broken down. In the night. Three tyres exploded in one day. Then also, they are fine. Just fine. They don't have things like exams to worry about. Like results. Like hanging themselves from the burglar guards. Like tomorrow. Even like yesterday. Just today, that's all they've got. Just today. And it's everything. This moment. They've got it. I ask myself if they are always like this.

No doubt about it.

I watch the water of the Belil River moving. Towards the sea, it drifts. Grand for so small a river. It passes, but is here, passes, but is here, on and on. I remember Captain now. 'Good luck,' he said, 'Good luck, Krish. Until your eighteenth.' So he knew. He knew all along. He took that risk.

Then, something else. He said: 'Consider yourself my younger brother. What d'you say, Kid, we take him as a younger brother?' Once again, between them I feel a certain love. And they have taken in the ugly duckling. On to their pond.

'Yeah, he's a good kid,' Kid said, looking up at Captain, sharing even his name with me.

'If I want to contact you, some time?' I asked.

'Not so easy,' Captain said, 'because I'm moving house next week. We owe too much rent, so we need to move on. Not to say get out of the place. Not to say escape. Not to mention a night-flit. We are moving on. It's time. There's a time for everything. One should never exaggerate things. Kid, as for him, Ruxana is about to chuck him out by the scruff of his neck. On grounds of drink. For her, those are grounds. So Kid may well be without fixed abode soon. SDF. *Sans domicile fixe*. But you can always come and see us in Pwentosab, everyone there knows Captain. And Kid's family name is Dilmamud. But I'd like to say just one more thing, if you'll permit. Let *me* rather take *your* address. We can come and see you one day, Krish. In the limousine.'

So, they *have* got hassles. Real ones. Rent unpaid and wives kicking them out. Real difficulties. Not ephemeral ones like exam results, little bits of paper pinned up on notice boards, pretending to sort out the good from the worthless. But look at them. I imagine my mother's face when they arrive in front of the house in Karo Lalyann.

'I am from Karo Lalyann.'

'Which house?'

'It's the only pink house, coconut-cake pink, my mother likes that colour, in Boundary Number One. Ask people for where Baya used to live. Baya who died young. Say you're looking for his little brother. That's me.'

They shake hands.

Kid squeezes my hand hard. 'You've got two brothers now. My condolences, Krish, for your big brother.' Then he smiles. 'But, careful, don't say goodbye to Major and Chanchal, they'll be too sad. They'll be sadder than sad monkeys.' He laughs at this. I am full of all sorts of emotions. Overwhelmed.

∗

I watch a bit of paper floating down the Belil River. *Ti bato papye.* Carry along my dreams, little paper boatlet, carry along my dreams. I see an old, old lady at the water's edge, or is it my imagination? She is leaning over the river. Her shawl is waft-lifted by the murmuring of the wind. Song words echo in my ears: *Mo truv enn vye bonnfam-la*. Is she fishing for little kabo? *Why! Why my children, must you work to earn your bread?* Then she disappears into the shadows of the riverbank, and I'm not sure she was ever there.

So I look up from the riverbank, put my chin up, and set off. I begin the long walk home. The first steps of a long walk. For me it might as well be the long march. However long, I must start it.

But, no, as it turns out, the march is not long. Not *that* march, anyway. Destiny wills otherwise.

Before I even get to Zefrwa Branch Road, I hear a car going in the same direction as me, hooting like mad, now pulling up right next to me. I look up. Unbelievable. Impossible. It's the limousine, with Captain and Kid in it, and the two dogs wagging their tails.

I must have been dreaming longer than I thought.

'We're going fishing tonight instead. Would you like to come with us?'

'Instead of what?' I think to myself. Captain then proceeds to invite me formally from behind the steering wheel, leaning over it, and looking up at me, and revving all the while. He is laughing out aloud.

The honour should be mine.

Kid is already out of the limousine and has tilted the car seat forwards for me, again standing there like a butler in a comedy film. While I stand there, thinking. Major and Chanchal wag their tails loudly against the back window, egging me on. This is my second invitation to go fishing. I have refused one already, and look where that led me. Consequences so drastic from such a petty decision. I hesitate as I think, once again, of the seasickness. Dismiss the thought as a stale one. I decide not to draw this out any longer.

'Yes, I'd like to,' I say, and climb in. I'll give fishing a try again, I say to myself, just to see if I get seasickness or not.

'Drive on, driver, drive on,' Kid sings, '*Rulé sofer, rulé*!'

So, on we drive. Once we are on the road, I build up my courage and launch into a confession, addressed to Captain.

'I've been in a pirogue once before. And that day I got seasick,' I venture.

Captain doesn't reply. He just puts his hand straight into the box on the inside of the Mini's door, under the door-opening string, and digs around amongst the papers there, pulling out a white paper packet, 'There you are,' his hand is up in the air with it, travel pills. 'I also take them. Kid never gets seasick in any case, but I do. When we stop moving forwards. Just watch out, if you drink beer with this pill, you'll go to sleep on the boat instead of catching fish.'

We arrive in the limousine at the fish-landing station at Pwentosab, where Captain parks carefully, clearly keeping in mind any later need for pushing. It's a reflex for him. There, sitting around in the fish-landing station kiosk that nestles in the enormous lakoklis trees glistening green, talking and drinking beer from the *lagul* of the bottle, is a group of young fishermen. We three shake hands with all of them in turn, and, like them, we take up seats on stones in that roughly drawn circle. One by one, each of them is telling a slow story. We get drawn in now. About a bad decision this one took one morning to go out in a sea so bad he should have known better. We listen to these tales. Tales of self-deprecation, gentle and kind, woven in with tales of obligatory heroism. It dawns on me now. Each of these lone fishermen avoids a certain death by the tiniest wrong decision, when he's gone out in a peanut shell of a pirogue, facing the cold and relentless swells they describe coming from the south, getting higher and higher, speeding his pirogue up on the downhill and slowing it down dangerously on the uphill, while at the same time from the other direction, the wind-chop's short-length waves of warm water from the north wrap around and get worse, threatening to overtake from behind and fill up his pirogue.

I, who fear seasickness, am bewitched. I, who fear everything under the sun, marvel. I am a child, playing man.

I feel each one's aloneness in the sea.

Alone as I am in the world.

And it is there that we meet up with a fisherman Captain and the Kid obviously know very well, called Jon-Jon, to whom they propose a joint outing. On the spot.

'It's almost no-moon,' he says, 'Do you want to go out anyway?'

'Yes,' Captain says. 'We won't fish for squid or anything. Nor trail lines, because that would need a moon. Just bottom-fishing will do. I've got a good torch to show us the way for getting back through the gap in the reef in the morning. Do you agree to take us then?'

Jon-Jon agrees to take us on a whole night's fishing. We'll share the catch, divide it in five, a share to each of the four of us, including Jon-Jon, and a second share for his boat. Naturally.

Captain and Kid tell me to wait at the fish-landing station, they'll be back straight away. They are going off to look for some bait on loan, they say, something I didn't know you could *borrow*. Maybe you can't, but they can. They think nothing of it. They also take Major and Chanchal home, to feed them and leave them. And they will grab warm clothes for themselves and for me, jerseys and gloves, and a packed supper each with a drink, including a thermos of hot black coffee with sugar in it against the cold.

The fishermen move on to low-key stories now. Two of the crack deep-sea fishermen have got very short wives. Another teases them: 'No easy task to take on, to find such tiny wives.' *Tigit marse zot ti bizin marse pu gayn madam tikalite kumsa.*

When Captain and Kid get back they are laughing uncontrollably. Captain explains. He says they don't know if his adversaries were spreading rumours or what other mischief someone was up to, but whatever the source of it, the talk had been going around: 'MP Bodnat's dishing out drink!' 'For MP Bodnat's birthday, he's paying for drinks!' 'Converge on the St Antoine *lakanbiz*!' 'MP Bodnat's handing out rum!' 'MP Bodnat invites one and all!' And so on.

Men from the housing estate, fishermen from all along the coast, and watchmen from the shacks behind rich people's bungalows, have all already come down to St Antoine's and are standing around. They are expecting drinks. They have formed groups on the beach and at the shop, waiting for MP Bodnat. MP Bodnat knows for a fact that if he appears on the scene under these circum-stances, he hasn't got any choice. He *has* to hand out free drinks.

Since this would be impossible to do, as the throng that has converged has now grown too big, he's had to go into hiding in self-defence. Everyone thinks it's hilarious. He had to abandon his BMW in the yard of his main electoral agent, and made an undignified escape in the ice-cream van that had turned up the road to the stone-crusher.

'What a way to lose your life, hey!' Captain remarks.

This was just a story in passing for Captain and Kid. An amusement.

Work must go on, though. Captain hands me an old jersey to put on and an old baby blanket that I can cover my knees with. Plus a striped knitted cap. Red and black. My ladybird. He and I each down a pill just in case, with a swig from the water bottle they've brought. Captain points out the pirogue we'll be going out in. It looks very, very small to me. It hasn't got a bridge on it at all. *Lakok pistas.* And I can just see those short-length waves from the northern wind-chop filling it up from behind.

I notice that Jon-Jon is bailing water out of it. Already. In the lagoon. Before we even hit the big sea. Imagine if the boat is anything like the limousine. But there's no way out of it now, for me. I'm stuck.

'Pump away, Jon-Jon,' Kid says, as though this bailing is normal, 'Pump away!'

Jon-Jon brings the pirogue to the lagoon's edge and we climb on board. Kid takes the punting stick, and propels the boat forwards by leaning on it. It's pitch dark. They know this bay like the back of their hands, I convince myself. When Kid has punted a few hundred yards, Jon-Jon pulls the cord of the outboard engine, and its motor springs gently to life. Captain looks at my face, then assures me there are sails in case of an engine failure. He makes a face as if to say he knows that I know how many mechanical failures there can be on one day. An infinite number. But this only makes me more worried because it hadn't entered my mind before that an *engine* might break down at sea. I was always too worried about the boat sinking or my being seasick to think of the real dangers. The sea, when I concentrate really hard, is, I realize, a domain without any motor mechanics. No Jaynan and his brother out there.

Outside the reef, when Jon-Jon finds a good place to fish on the way to Albion, he cuts out the engine, lets down an anchor, and the boat sits there. A silence, broken only by the lap-lap-lapping of the sea against the side of the pirogue, licking her affectionately. And the flare of the odd match being struck to light a cigarette. A sweet, calm silence. And we prepare.

'So, you gonna tell us how you line her up here then, Skipper?' Kid asks Jon-Jon. But Jon-Jon just laughs. 'It's a trade secret,' Captain whispers loudly to me.

Jon-Jon hands me my own fishing nylon, wound in a perfect thick figure of eight around a wooden stick. As though this is usual. But I'm having difficulty with it. At the end of the nylon there are four or five treacherous hooks, each of which I have to bait, one by one. Trying not to be squeamish, I thread the smelly old bits of squid on to the hooks. When I foul-hook myself a second time, and before I do it so badly a third time that they have to do a cut-down with the bait knife to get the hook out, Kid comes over and helps me out. They explain everything to me as we go along, not because they are charitable, I can tell, but to stop me spoiling the night in some way or other, through my ignorance.

In particular, they tell me that if they all find they've got to move to one side because of any problem that might arise, whether minor or a grave danger, then I've got to move to the *other* side at once, if I please. If they go starboard, I must go port. If they go port, I must go starboard.

All this terrifies me even more.

Later, we get out our picnic and settle in to a feast. This calms my fears. I get very hungry when I'm out at sea, I decide. White rice, tomato chutney with chillies and onions, leaf soup, and mutton and potato as a dry curry, with mint in it. We drink a beer each. They take me as one of them. And we fish. We fish in silence. In darkness. In peace. Just some phosphorus on the edges of the odd wave, rippling jewels lining a triangular shawl being thrown over a shoulder. That's what I see.

And I feel safe. In a boat too small for the big sea. In water too deep for me to estimate. With three men I've only just met.

Safe.

Jon-Jon catches the first fish. A four-pounder, he says, a Captain fish which Captain says he ought to have caught, it being his namesake. But he picks up a fine Karang instead. I try to see the difference, but they both look like fish to me.

'Look at the bulge on the Captain fish's head,' Captain says, showing me the difference.

Despite my pill and my beer, it is only around midnight that I fall fast asleep. Still holding my line in my right hand, I lie there oblivious to everything. The others fish on. I hear their slow talk when I wake up, with no consonants in it, only vowels, and then I doze off again.

Each time I wake up, the sea is still calm. No wind either. A late summer sea, they say. But I wouldn't know.

In the morning, before the sun comes up, the sky goes red for a while. A sheen of red. Again. *Red sky in the morning, shepherd's warning.* Each mountain is like a cut-out in black, pasted on to cracker-red paper.

Jon-Jon announces it. We must begin to bring in the

lines now. Kid shows me how to wind mine up in a figure of eight, so that the ball of nylon is all round like a big oval ball. When I get my lines in, I find I've foul-hooked some kind of eel. 'Not going back on shore empty-handed anyway,' Jon-Jon laughs.

I'm so chuffed, you wouldn't believe it. A fucking eel.

We put everything away, shipshape for the return through the pass, the gap in the reef, and into the lagoon. Tired, ready to go and sleep all day on the firm land. I think of Karo Lalyann, dreading this particular bit of firm land. The devil or the deep blue sea?

I now can't think why exam results ever seemed so important to anyone, especially to me.

Then we see another pirogue inside the lagoon, approaching us.

'That's Augustin's pirogue,' Jon-Jon announces, 'Look, he and his wife are out fishing together again. Takes all sorts.'

Silence as we watch them. The other three are watching, but pretending not to be watching.

'Funny, he seems to be signalling us something,' Jon-Jon says, already concerned. As if a fisherman would never ever dream of signalling another fisherman to come over unless there was a catastrophe. Some kind of admission of defeat.

'Yes, that's so,' Captain confirms it. 'He is calling us over. Get nearer then, Jon-Jon.'

As we approach, we move over shallow waters. No more than two or three feet, full of treacherous corals. We get nearer and the lagoon gets shallower. Jon-Jon turns off the engine, and tilts it into the boat so that the rudder and propeller are safely up in the air. It's very shallow now, and Kid, without a word from Jon-Jon, takes up the punting stick again, goes to the front tip of the pirogue, leans on it and propels us onwards in silence. Now he is also like a black cut-out against the red sky. Until we are abreast of Augustin's pirogue.

Augustin seems upset. His wife does too. We can read it in their gestures, even before they say anything. Some sort of trouble. Grave trouble. But what?

'Look over here,' he says pointing into the lagoon, 'Just come and look at this. Yes, look into the water.'

I am on the same side as Captain. When we get near enough, Augustin is still pointing. We will see before Jon-Jon and Kid do. They stay on the other side, so as not to unbalance the boat. We will look first.

I don't want to look, but I have to. It's my duty now. That's how much my life has changed. It is my duty to look into the water.

The first rays of sun come up, slitting the sky diagonally like a blade, and making the red sky look like blood. *Red sky in the morning, shepherd's warning.*

Under the water, in the shallows, lit by those first rays, I see it. It is a dead body. A young girl. Her body just lying there, as though she is asleep on her back. Except that there's this heavy rock tied to her chest, weighing her down. Both her arms are swishing left and right, as if she is trying to explain something a bit complicated. But it's only the swells moving them. Her arms are only moving to the very same rhythm as the seaweed around her. As if they are all dancing, she and her seaweed-cloaked friends. Her small bare feet are tied together with an orange ribbon. A long evening dress, in thin, light orange-coloured material, clings to her, except for the loose wide collar that moves like a shawl, and the skirt-edge, which swirls in the water. A mermaid, I think. It's a mermaid. A pearl earring in each ear lobe. Pearls to pearls. Her thick hair moving gently with the waves. Just like all the mauve seaweed around her. A symphony of silence. A symphony of fear.

'No!' Captain cries in a strangled voice. 'No. *Mo pa'le krwar*. They've killed her. Someone's killed the young prostitute. No more than a child. And thrown her into the sea. The new girl.'

'What should we do?' Jon-Jon asks. He knows the problems ahead, that's for sure.

Augustin does too. So he says: 'What with my wife being with me, it's more difficult . . . you know.' Captain angers. 'If you don't want to help, then fuck off. Fuck right off. You and your goddamned wife.'

'Don't talk that way, Captain,' Jon-Jon pleads, 'in front of a lady.'

'We come over when you call us. We come over to help you out. And you are too cowardly to stay. Any fool knows there's trouble for us in this. Get the hell out of here, then!' Captain goes on. 'And fast!'

'Don't involve me in it,' Augustin adds, making sure, 'Not in any part of it. That will only complicate it and make it take even longer for us all to get out.'

I don't know what they are talking about. *Get out of what?*

I just stay gazing at her. Gawping. I can't believe it. The mermaid of Pwentosab. A mermaid posing for a photograph. A mermaid, lying down because she is suddenly very tired. Resting, just for a short while. Her pale-orange dress and mock pearls. Then, for a few minutes, I wait, I wait for her to smile and sit up and say, 'Only a bit of theatre,' and to throw the horrid rock off her chest, and to leave the dangerous orange ribbon round her ankles. She will turn over and swim away. With her ankles tied together like that, she would have to swim like a dolphin. Because, after all, she is a mermaid.

Drowning. Death by drowning. Murder. Assassination. Premeditation. A body. A corpse. Dead. Lost. And so young.

Like my Baya. I'm short-circuited again. Lost as Baya.

We have found her, but we can't get her back again. And then again, she looks about to sit up and say, 'There you are now, I'm back again.' But no, she is dead as dead can be. She is completely submerged. She is underwater, her nose filled with seawater, a rock on her chest. Or am I imagining all this? She's just pretending. She will come back to life.

Augustin turns his back on us, and goes. Punts his pirogue away. He and his wife. Out of the story. Heads bowed in some shame. I can't work out what shame.

Captain and Jon-Jon, one from each side, get out of the pirogue and stand in the water. It's up to their thighs. A strange sadness in their every movement. In not more than three foot of water. Captain becomes more businesslike and leans over, putting first his arms and then his whole head right under the water. He pulls the rock off her chest, untying it at the same time. It turns out not to be a rock at all, but an iron thing, the engine block of a small vehicle. And suddenly, her head and shoulders float up, so young a girl suddenly sitting up in the sea, in her orange dress, almost trying to stand. As though she had come back to life. Captain pulls his head out of the water, as if scared by her sudden movement. But he controls himself. Again he has to plunge his head and shoulders underwater, so as to untie an iron ball from underneath her tied bare feet. He stays under for ages, maybe a full minute, holding his breath as he undoes the pale orange ribbon. She floats now. The whole of her. Macabre in the newly risen sun. The lagoon so blue. The coral so silver. Her skin so metal grey. Her black eyes open wide. Accusing. Her flimsy orange dress moving on the surface of the lagoon now.

Captain and Jon-Jon slowly lift her, ever so carefully, with respect due to her, and hand her into the arms of Kid and me. We have to lean right over as we take her, although she is light, so very light. Then we put her down on the floorboards of the pirogue. Captain and Jon-Jon climb back in again.

'Innocent,' Captain says. 'Poor devil. Poor angel.' He bites his lower lip. He lifts his head up to the sky, as if to ask for an answer to his accusations. Then he leans down and firmly closes her eyes. Holds them closed.

'Do you know her? Is she a Pwentosab girl?' I ask.

'No, not really. I've just seen her once. She's a new girl.'

When he lets go her eyes, they open again. Again they accuse us.

Jon-Jon acts resigned.

Accepting of such things.

He says: 'Let's just go to the police right away, and see what they do with us. We'll try and talk some sense into them, though what's the point really. What's the time?' It's as though he is already preparing for the formal enquiry. 'Get our bearings exactly. Remember who got out the pirogue and who stayed in. Which fish you each caught. Or which bloody eel. Which side of which bench you fished from. What colour fucking cap you are each fucking wearing.'

'Watch your language,' Captain insists, dull voiced.

'It'll be eleven o'clock before we even get inside the police station,' Kid replies, 'All of this has taken time, and is still taking time, and will take even more time. For a start, we have to punt all the way over to the police station. It's the safest thing to do.'

*

The police officers stand on the dry sand, watching the spectacle. We lift her off the pirogue on to the sand. They wouldn't want to wet their boots, I can see. Then, they announce, with regret they say, that they are naturally arresting all of us on the spot. There and then. Without further ado.

The inspector takes delivery of the girl's body, by making two constables wrap her up in a sheet they get sent to fetch, out of propriety, from the station. They carry her body into the police station without ceremony. Meanwhile the sergeant is loudly telephoning the police draughtsman, the police photographer, and also the police doctor for the autopsy. The inspector gives orders for the pirogue to be searched. They impound our catch. There goes my eel, I think. Then we are marched to the police station ourselves. All our bags are taken from us for searching and impounding. We are herded into the cell, the grille is closed, and the padlock locked loudly.

Just like that.

A run-of-the-mill arrest. No supplementary questions asked. No time wasted.

Captain protests, on our behalf. But this is normal, so they take no notice of us or of his protests. In any case, there is such disorder in the police station that closing four people up tidies things up a bit. 'That's better,' the Inspector mumbles, 'Nice and clean.'

Captain mumbles: 'In case trouble breaks out later. A riot. Or a *breaking in by band*. A revolt. A revolution. Whichever way, they seem to know full well what public order they are in charge of establishing, what peace they are in charge of maintaining.'

It's all there out of habit. I've clicked. For them it's all routine, bureaucratic routine. They don't do anything in particular to us. They haven't got anything against us. So they mainly just lock us up and ignore us. I watch all this, as if it were a film, as if I weren't in it. This is how these police officers see us: There is a body. We found it. It was in Pwentosab. (We did not ever mention the Augustin bit. He was right, of course, Augustin was. It would only make it more complicated. Nor do we mention his wife.) We brought the body to the police station. We name no suspects. There are no other suspects. Therefore we must be locked up in the cell. We found the body, so we are the first suspects. It stands to reason.

So there we are, locked up in the police cell.

Underneath I am shit-scared. But I watch Captain.

He keeps his calm. So we all follow suit, and keep ours. He even takes the time to tell us a story or two. For light relief.

But despite all this, I get time to reflect, in scraps of time between events and stories, on my day and my night. The smallest lie about leaving Mamu's at four o'clock, a detour through hitchhiking, a humble fishing outing, a beer or two, and I find myself locked up in a police cell.

It is the easiest thing for them to do, lock us up. Path of least resistance.

But nevertheless, a nuisance. We are a nuisance to them. You can see the way they look at us and sigh. Given half a chance they would hit us. If the press or politicians raise any outcry against this poor girl's killer, they'll use this as a reason to put our heads into hoods and hit us with thick sticks. I remember this from newspaper articles. At the time I read these things, it was as if they were happening on Mars. If they decide we have to confess, they will tie us to pylons and put lit candles under the soles of our feet until we do. This, too, I remember reading. It never entered my head that this could happen to me. I must have been on Mars before.

The policemen hold a conversation amongst themselves. Shabbily. Soon, *as the day progresses*, they say these words with scorn, *as the day progresses*, the cell in Pwentosab will *fill up*. It's that kind of place, they moan. They grumble. Fill up, as it is wont to do. Like the diurnal tide coming in. And by night-time, it'll be chock-a-block. So, to make space for later arrests, they might as well *not* take statements from us here, and instead just transfer us straight to the Banbu police cells. 'Therefore, they can give their statements *there*,' they say, thus passing the buck. Even I can see that.

Unquestionable logic in it. So we stay locked up all day listening to a few more stories from Captain. Waiting. I ask permission to go to the toilets. It is accorded, and I am escorted there and back by a policeman who smells of fear. It does not enter my mind to flush anything down the toilet. The contents of the cellophane packet, tiny in the recesses of my pocket, are completely buried in the recesses of my mind. Forgotten.

Later Ruxana, Kid's wife, brings us all four food in two *catora*. And a litre of tea in a Coke bottle. The policemen tell her she can't talk to us. Jon-Jon's mother brings us a bag of deep-fried bringal cakes and quarters of pineapple with chilli and salt. She tells the police to watch it, she's got a lawyer she'll get in. I realize she is protecting us from something by this threat. And I'm pretty sure what.

At six o'clock sharp, they unlock our cell, jostle us out. One of them carries our bags, the other one handcuffs us in two pairs, and shoves us into the back of a police jeep. Me and Captain. Jon-Jon and Kid. There is a sergeant in front next to the driver, with our bags on his lap now, and a constable with us at the back.

We all set off for Banbu, where it is not inevitable that the cell will be full by the end of the night.

On the way the sergeant turns around to us in the back and announces it, 'You will be brought before the magistrate there tomorrow morning.' He makes it sound like we are being accorded a special privilege, as if we should be appreciative. Next time we might not get this treatment. And then, as if to show his infinite power over us, he adds, 'Or the next day.'

'Tell your families to get bail ready. I'd expect it to be around five thousand.'

I shake my head, sitting there in that jeep, handcuffed to Captain. I start mumbling to myself: 'Where will these events lead to? I'm in trouble now. Deep trouble. In cells overnight. In court tomorrow for bail. Charges of what? Of murder? Is this how life goes?' I am in a state of shock. Utter and complete. I never knew life was like this.

Captain realizes, and puts his non-handcuffed hand on my shoulder, 'I'm sorry,' he says, 'Apologies for all this.

'And where are we supposed to get hold of five thousand, sergeant?' Captain says, all calm and rational, making an art of keeping the banter going. Keeping our spirits up. Keeping us feeling like humans, humans who can negotiate. When I'm so dazed I've given up.

I reply to Captain now, playing the reassuring one: 'It's

not our fault. We aren't guilty of anything.' When we speak to each other, it's in low tones, so that even the constable next to us in the back can't be sure what we are saying. Which makes him look at us with distaste. Four habitual criminals so close to him he can't get away from us. 'If you were in the USA, you'd have leg shackles on you by now! So watch it!'

'What exactly is the USA to you, then, sir, your mother's husband?' Captain asks this, as if curious about a precise family tree.

All I've ever known in my life up to now seems dull. Pale, boring, tasteless. It even seems to have a ring of something false to it. How was it that before now I didn't know that this was how life goes on, day to day, in this country? On this planet? A young girl's dying like that. Murdered? Bodies disposed of in the lagoon like that? A corpse without a name. And when law-abiding citizens, good Samaritans even, bring the body ashore, hand it over to the police, they get arrested on the spot? And threatened with leg irons.

'And they've got the death penalty there too,' the policeman adds. The girl in the newspaper, caught in that granular photograph, comes back to me.

'Shalt not envy thy neighbour!' Captain mocks him. The policeman looks at his boots.

Captain whispers into my ear again: 'When we told that Augustin fellow and his wife to get the hell out of it, we knew what was coming to us. But we're not stupid. You see we haven't got any other choice, really. And it's true his wife would have also had to be locked up. Augustin is OK, a good man, really, even though we cursed him. His wife's also a good woman. But they are scared of everything. Scared of the police. Scared of the courts. Scared of death.

Scared of scandal. Scared of ghosts. What can you do then, if you're like that, if you're scared all the time? You give in. That's what you do. You submit.

'And so, they make a practical calculation, they do. Either they get all the problems or we do. So they prefer us to. But for people like us, we don't have that choice, do we? We can't just shift the problems on to someone else, just to get ourselves off the hook. Can we? Poor dead girl. A child. Did you look at her? A child. Same age as you I'd put her. And even when she's dead no one will take her side. Except maybe us. The least we can do.' Again the grainy photograph of the other girl, the condemned girl. From faraway shores. Hanged by the neck until. Or held under water until. Or was this girl not drowned, but killed first, and only then put under the water of the lagoon, so as to get rid of the body? What thoughts invade me. I see myself now, drowned in my own bodily fluids, with a bottle of orange mineral water glinting on the window ledge, in my own mental secretions.

Captain goes on: 'But for you, Krish, it isn't the same. Just because you were with us, it isn't fair on you. You were no more than our guest, so it's not fair and it's not right. That's why I say I'm sorry.

'In any case, even if we didn't do it for *her* – she's dead now anyway and gone, nothing can be done for her really – we still didn't have much choice. Our pirogue was near the site. People would have seen us there. The police would have made someone tell them we were near there. Then, if we hadn't acted like we did, we would have been in for far bigger problems, I can tell you. If we hadn't brought the body in ourselves, we'd be done. Then even lawyers wouldn't have got us off. Not even Gaetan Duval, if he was still alive. Fucking pimps, they would have had us set up with the murder charges. And the charges would have stuck like superglue, because we hadn't come and handed in the body. So we are only acting in self-interest, when you think about it. Unfortunately, we can't claim anything more than that, Krish.'

I believe Captain is a hero, of course.

I shudder as I think of my mother and father's reaction. They would deduce the worst. Their little boy. Their little baby boy. Their '*Boy!*' Would they cry? Snivel? Complain? Their boy accused of killing a Pwentosab prostitute? And his defence is that he was set up by Pwentosab pimps? They would be lost. They wouldn't know what to do. They are even less prepared for life than I am.

I feel the short circuit coming. Here it comes: If only I had died in Baya's place.

If only. If only I had died instead. If he had lived instead of me, he wouldn't have put them to all this trouble. That's for sure. My mother and father could have been proud of their son. Instead of having to bail him out of the Banbu lock-up, when he's on murder charges, involved with a prostitute and pimps.

They will think all sorts of things. That I have always been telling them lies about everything. That I was bunking school every other day. That I am a bandit, smoking gandya, eating sausages and living barefaced lies day in day out, in their house in Karo Lalyann.

And my mother will think everything can be sorted out through some practical arrangement. Maybe through influence. Through money. Through some distant and high-up family member. Through a minister. That's how she thinks the world is, my mother. She just thinks she's the only one in the world who doesn't have these strings to pull. Everyone else has got them. Everyone else, according to her, has got *backing*. Everyone else has got *influence*. Sometimes she even prays to the gods that she could get hold of a bit of backing, a bit of influence. Just a little bit of influence. For exams, her main worry was how to get hold of exam papers before the exam. No matter how much I told her it wasn't good, and wasn't right, and wasn't possible, she went on that other kids did it.

Which is a known fact. With the help of their parents. Though I don't know how they do it.

And my father?

But I am perplexed here. He is, after all, a taxi driver. They know these things, taxi drivers do. It's part of their profession, isn't it? Prostitutes and pimps use taxis. That's how they get around. Taxi drivers guide clients to them. Everyone knows that. Quacks and touts use taxis, too. And taxi drivers direct people to them for further direction to specialists in healing illnesses of the eyes, heart, spleen, and in the removal of unwanted pregnancies, specialists in getting people off charges of burglary, receiving stolen goods and rape, in corrupting the appropriate policemen, and in pulling out teeth without a licence. Even I know all this. Somewhere at the back of my narrow mind, I know it.

Is it just that I was under the impression that my father doesn't know about all these things? A misapprehension I had. Or did he keep them in a separate part of his mind? Or maybe he isn't that kind of taxi driver, he is one who drives slowly and by the law, carting around old ladies and mothers with sick children, that's why he can't get enough money to buy a new car like all the others seem to be able to.

Suddenly, all at once, I come to my senses. It hits me. From some hidden part of *my* mind.

I am in deep trouble.

Genuine panic starts to invade me now. I begin to realize, it starts to dawn on me. There is something else. Something disastrous. It is *me* who was under some misapprehension about things. I am the one who acts like an ignorant fool. I slowly put my free hand down to my trouser pocket. *Fool's errand*, that's what. Hidden in a separate part of my body. I, Boy alias Krish, I am sitting here in a police jeep, I am about to be locked up in police cells in the Banbu police station, and in my trouser pocket, I have a measure of grass. A *puliah*. Marihuana. A drugs case. Why didn't I throw it away earlier in the toilet? Or leave it in the Pwentosab cell? Which means, even if the others get released, I will not. I am now suspect number one. A drug user. A drug abuser. A drug addict. It all gets amalgamated. It will all be added up against me. And they'll ask me where I got it. And they'll beat me up until I say. And then they'll go and get *him* for dealing, my Mamu Dip.

It's clear. It's evident. A crime, and I am guilty of it.

Maybe I'll have to make out I'm the dealer myself, to save Mamu Dip. And they'll have me for hanging. Along with the girl from India. By my neck, till I die.

I am the same as her.

Two errands. We are *errands*. She for an unscrupulous boss. Me for a self-centred, silly-headed mother.

Captain notices that the expression on my face has changed.

'Don't worry,' he whispers, 'we'll get you a lawyer when we get to the Banbu police station. They have to let us use the phone for that.' Not for himself, he won't get a lawyer. But for *me*. 'Lawyers are a race of bastards all right, but you're too young to go and get previous. We'll take a lawyer for you. I've got one. I've got one I'm on good terms with.' He whispers this last phrase in an upper-class accent, looking arrogantly around the jeep. He's already talking about previous. What I will have got in my past. I, a future has-been.

When we get to the Banbu police station, the policeman in the back with us shoos us out of the jeep. Like we are vermin. With disgust. I watch the way Captain and I, made into twins, Siamese twins, manoeuvre ourselves with elegance. I smile. A closer brother than this I could not hope for.

As I'm going in I look down, head bowed with worry about what's in my pocket more than anything else, and what do I see? To my wonder, I see, and nearly trip over, a beautiful little garden, miniature, in front of the police station, full of plants in hectic flowering abundance. Perfume giddies me. Ah yes, newspaper article yesterday morning when I was sitting on the steps drinking my tea after getting my results, just after that granular photograph of the mysterious girl from India: '*Jardin d'un poste de police: Premier prix à Bambous.*' All kinds of flowers shining up at the sun. Incredible but true. I almost fall over, because my other half is certainly not wasting his time looking at flowers in any flower bed. Geraniums and perfume geraniums, whose leaves breathe wonder into the air, sunflowers yellow around black in back rows, coral flowers of every tinkling pale colour right in the front, spilling over on to the stone path, and double poinsettias so red on the outside you could cry, gladioli, yellow roses just opening. Ridiculously beautiful. Tended to with much more care than we are getting.

Nor do the flowers stop the police there from shoving us past, herding us and prodding us, pushing us around, making us cower. But then again, maybe if there weren't any flowers, maybe they would have been rougher, more brutish, who knows?

I have time to think all this.

'Hurry up. Get into the lock-up! At once. Chop, chop! Get in there!' One policeman pushes me so hard I almost fall over on the pathway between the two halves of the police station flower garden, making me tug hard on Captain's arm. But he steadies me with his free arm. 'Careful, brother,' he says. I see a policeman's right boot hovering in the air behind me, no weight on it. It is in readiness to kick me if I should by chance trip and fall. Which is why Captain already had his guard up.

As we pass the counter, on our way through to the lock-up, Captain signals me that we're stopping, and he leans over on the counter: 'I need to ring my lawyer, James Bronson. Pass me the telephone, if you don't mind. Pardon? Or you can dial for me. I am encumbered, as you can see. He won't be at the office any more. It's half past six.' Captain says all this as though he is in charge around here. And yet politely. It actually *is* half past six. '240 3427,' he adds, 'You dial for me.' The policeman duly dials.

Luckily the lawyer is at home. He says, yes, he'll take my case. He'll be around to see me tomorrow morning, after his case in the Second Division in Porlwi. I am to wait for him, please, and not to give any statement or anything until he comes. Then, in his presence, I can give my statement, he says. It's too late to get me out today, he says, because the charges will be too heavy. Murder involved.

'Now get your assholes in there at once.' The policeman is losing patience with us, troublemakers with lawyers. I sense it.

We will have to go in. And as we get nearer, I see the

police are preparing to search us. Body search. One on each side of the grille.

I'm a goner. My life is well and truly fucked up. Fucked right up. Swearing is a detail now.

Captain feels my panic, we are still sharing one arm after all. I suddenly feel him stop, halt in his tracks, while I have taken a step forward, and I hear his voice just behind me, 'I have something important to say to the inspector, if you don't mind. Could he be called for me, please? Or could you take me and this boy to see him, if you prefer?' He is playing a wild card. Even I know that. 'An outsider's chance,' he leans over and whispers in my ear.

At that very moment, and Captain had seen him coming, the inspector is coming into the room, and starts picking up this and that, clearly preparing to go off duty. *Luck sometimes has to go our way. Pure chance.* He picks up his tatty briefcase in his right hand, and his empty lunch basket in his left hand. Like a child going home from primary school, it strikes me. *Home to mummy.*

'What charges on these detainees?' he queries, hardly taking us into his glance at all.

The sergeant stands up and replies, 'Brought in the body of some woman. Found it in the lagoon at Pwentosab. *Enn pitin.* Foul play. Someone's killed a prostitute. We haven't got the cause of death yet. The body's at the Kandos morgue.' I think of the mortuary I went past yesterday morning. I think of the dead girl's body lying still on the tiles of the dissecting table. I shudder. I see her hair waving in the sea, the mauve seaweed mixed into it.

'And these are what exactly? Suspects?' He casts a glance at us, both neutral and disgusted. '*Prime* suspects?' Like grades of meat.

'They've got some story or other. Supposedly they were

just doing night-fishing near there and they came across the body, just *came across* it on their way back in. But this one,' he points out Kid, ahead of us, 'he's got previous. And the boat owner, he's got a conviction for using a gill net out of season. Which means he's also got previous. And in any case, we haven't got anyone else. Not yet anyway.'

'Exactly, inspector,' Captain chimes in. 'If I may add something. There happens to be with us someone who is *under age*.' Captain makes this sound like a very clear category that policemen know about, 'Let him leave his name and address and go home. No need to bar a place in the lock-up room, is there now? He was our guest. We took him out fishing. To cheer him up. He doesn't know anything about anything. Look at him. Could be anyone's son,' Captain means *he could be your son*. 'He is too young to be locked up with grown men. Recidivists and all. Look at me, I haven't got previous, but you can lock me up. But let this kid go.' And for good luck, with the gentlest hint of a threat of some sort, he adds, 'Don't make us have to make a meal out of this.'

'Your age, then?' the inspector asks.

'Seventeen,' I answer.

'Where d'you work?'

'I've just finished exams.' He looks at me properly now. An additional distaste. A privileged child getting up to no good, worse still. Spoilt.

'Take his name and address, sergeant, a detailed address please,' he says, 'and let him go. Keep these three. Give them a night to think about things in peace and quiet before they tell us what happened. Bloody women. Getting up to no good. If she were in my household, I'd teach her. Let this little squirt go home to his mummy.' The very words I had thought of about *him*.

Captain is more pleased than even I am. His smile radiates all around that police station. He almost looks for applause. That's what he's like. He is getting locked up, and he is celebrating the fact that I'm not.

I'm so relieved I could die. But Captain doesn't even know why.

Captain leans over to me and says, 'Leave aside court tomorrow, you are invited to come and visit us in Pwentosab this coming weekend. If we aren't still locked up. And don't worry too much about the dead girl. She is, unfortunately, it's sad I know, but she is dead already. If you want to worry about someone, worry about someone like her who's still alive, will you. That's my advice.'

I never realized how clear Captain's thinking was. I feel in him a criticism of my mother and father.

Of me, even. His ideas make me feel as if mine are immoral. *Like my mother's*. Mine have never had that kind of refinement.

The police bring along the keys and undo our handcuffs. Captain at once makes use of this new freedom to turn around towards me, and quite formally and solemnly to shake my hand. 'Don't you go worrying about us in here. Our families will bring us some food and cigarettes. Everyone in Pwentosab will know what's happened, and will take our side in this. People will go and get land deeds to use instead of bail money. No problem.'

Kid and Jon-Jon come over to shake my hand, each one offering whichever hand is free.

They are dignified. In chains, and yet dignified. Whereas I, a free man, lack all signs of dignity.

I am like a badminton cock. Being battered around by fate. *Sapsiway*.

I am a prisoner, even without the chains.

'You turn up here and report to me personally, eight-thirty tomorrow morning,' the inspector says, 'Pass you in front of the magistrate, with these here *friends* of yours.'

The policeman who came with us in the jeep says rudely: 'Which one is yours then?' And I point to my denim bag. He opens it up and searches it. He reads the inscription on the bangle out loud: *Balmick Burton*. Out loud.

'And who is *he*?' he asks.

'Was. Who *was* he,' I reply.

'Answer me, Smartarse!'

'My brother.'

I take my bag from him, put the bangle back in it, and turn away and leave.

*

So, I find myself back at the exact same place I was at yesterday. It wasn't much later than this time of day either. Talk about going round in circles.

On this immense planet called Earth, I have come back to the same place I was at yesterday. Snakes and ladders. Landing wherever the dice send me. Sometimes going up, other times coming down.

Or, as though there is some magnetism under the earth at this exact place, causing me to come back here. Maybe gravity is stronger here. Or there's some pole of attraction.

I stand on the edge of the road opposite the same Banbu police station again. Only now I know it. I leave three friends in it.

Again I watch the Belil River flow by. It is still here, that river. Lazy and making progress. The thick sonz leaves, giant elephant ears, nuzzling one another. *Why! Why, my children, why have to work to earn your bread?* The song again.

And how much water has flowed by?

How different I feel now. Am I not the same person who was here yesterday?

My internal landscape, the map of my mind, my inner self, my inbuilt compass, my soul's guide, all these things I didn't even know I had, are now not the same any more. Everything has changed. Gone disorganized, into turmoil, into flux.

But I can't just stand here, denim bag over my shoulder again, looking at the Belil River for ever. I will either have to catch a bus home, or walk. Or do something else. I can't just stand here.

In my sadness and my loss. I, like Augustin and his wife, turning my back on them. I, running an errand for my mother. On orders. I, a link in a chain of hypocrisy.

So I walk.

Then I walk a bit faster towards the road up to Kat Born. It is dark. Pitch dark. I've completely forgotten that there won't be a moon at all. Last night it was almost pitch dark, but I am not in touch with the world around me enough to remember *that*. I don't feel the rhythms of the moon in me.

So, I turn up Zefrwa Branch Road on foot.

A certain spring comes into my step. Sad, upset, confused, but buoyant. *The boy is buoyant*, I think. I start to laugh. At myself. I, the ridiculous.

I send my hand, instinctively now, towards my pocket. Just to check. It's still there. Twice nearly caught out. A shivering comes over me. And a cold sweat. The consequences of something so small. So small it fits unnoticed into my jeans pocket. The mere presence of a tiny bit of grass folded into a bit of cellophane paper twisted at one end. To be used with milk and spices in order to get closer to the gods.

And with this *closer to the gods*, the mermaid comes back to me, floating like that under the water. Died young. Like my Baya. No more than a child. Now the granular black-and-white photograph. Another girl. No more than a child, lost on her way from India. Same age as me. Tonight alone in the Bobasin prison. Just the other side of this mountain that presses like a dark shadow, darker than everything else, on my left side. Second night, after the verdict. Awaiting sentence. I touch my trouser pocket again. I, so close to this girl. Nothing separates us. She her boss's messenger. Me my mother's.

Now my elbows feel the weight of the mermaid in my arms, as Captain and Jon-Jon handed her up into the pirogue. So light, she was. No more than a child. I try to separate her from the girl in the prison. She is gone. To the girl in prison, I send warming thoughts. She's still alive. *Take care of the ones who are still alive.* In a strange land, full of strange people speaking strange languages, and applying strange laws. I, who don't even know her, *feel* for her. I, too, live in a strange land, full of strange people speaking strange languages, and applying strange laws. I, bearing with me a bit of wild weed, illegal to have in your pocket. Hang a girl like this? And for the mermaid, are the tiles in the mortuary cold? Why did she die? At whose hand? Who tied her feet? What pale-orange ribbon?

And my mind skids off again: Couldn't I have died in her place? Couldn't I die instead of the girl in the prison? Couldn't I have died in Baya's place? Why, oh, why did he have to die? I, the record stuck in a groove, I am. Not like the Belil River that quietly moves on, in graceful progress. I, obsessed, repetitive, ridiculous. Treading water fretfully.

I see the marks of the turquoise rope still on my neck. After my death. I see an article, modest and chill: '*ACTE DE DESESPOIR. Le même jour que les résultats des examens de la HSC, un jeune homme se livre à un acte de désespoir. Foul play n'est pas . . .*'

Why don't I act.

Finish all these thoughts that go round and round, repeating themselves, torturing me.

Strange when I think of it, it's so factual. An act. A blade. A snake of rope. A plastic bag . . . An action with a finite result.

If I ask myself *why do it?*, I answer myself *why not?*

The answer to *why not?*

The shadow of the mountain on the left side looms heavier now. Darker than dark. A presence. No sign of stars or planets on it. Just blackness. A black rug. That may slip, and cascade down on to me. Crush me. Knock the wind out of me. Smother me. Until there is no life left in me.

'Which would be good,' I say aloud. Aneantized.

Suddenly I have it. There is something that has changed. Here and now, as I walk.

Because of the girl walking up the hill at Kandos.

But I don't even know her. Her eyes so alive, so concentrated on me. She makes me exist.

So I walk on.

Like a new birth. My head tilts forwards and it's like a first step. One foot in front of the other. So I don't fall over, I put a foot out.

I won't die, I'm here to stay, life goes on. As I begin to face up to the night, I feel fear begin to trickle down the back of my neck. Coldly, I observe the fear in me. It begins, at the same time, to rise up inside me now, breaking out on to my skin. Everywhere. Goose bumps of fear on my neck, now my arms. A thrill of fear.

I admit it. I am afraid. What to do?

How can I turn up home to my mother and father's in Karo Lalyann at midnight? With a court case to announce to them? *Pass you before the magistrate.* A long court case starting. And going on and on until the faraway horizon. A bleak horizon. I can't even contemplate it. What will my mother think? What will my father say? What will my mother do? What will I tell them? I am not one for long explanations, all drawn out. I can't face that kind of thing. Cross-questioning from my mother, no I can't bear it. When I'll be sitting on the bench of the accused.

And even if I half-run, even if the sky miraculously lights up and I hurry all the way, there's no way I'll arrive home at a reasonable hour. Better I face a night outdoors on my own.

But this is only a vague idea to me, this night outdoors on my own. And this vagueness makes me even more scared. I don't even know what I'm scared of. Am I scared of wild animals? Am I scared of spirits? Or of people? Or of the unknown? What could there be in the dark out there that I should be afraid of?

Soon I work it out. It's obvious. I should stop along the way and find a place to shelter from the cold of the night, yes, a chill has crept into the air. The moon has shown no sign of putting in an appearance. Naturally.

Pitch dark, it is. My luck. I can see nothing. I can see no one. It strikes me how lucky I am that no one can see me either.

*

So, with each step I take, I place a foot down carefully, checking that I am still on the road, and not going off on to the verge, before transferring my weight on to it. I must avoid falling into a culvert, or a drain, or a canal. I must avoid bumping into anything, a tree, a pylon, or an unlighted vehicle.

There is a bright light way ahead. The stone-crusher's. Way ahead on Montan Bol. It doesn't help at all. Makes it more difficult to see nearby. Blinds me.

I miss Major and Chanchal. Who would have thought I could ever miss them? How much I cursed them and their ancestors. They would be company for me now, they would. I begin to think fondly of them. The first dogs I've ever known. They could have been guiding me, showing me the way. Dogs can see at night. They can warn you of things.

When I get the chance, I'll get myself a dog, I think. A puppy. *A person who wants a puppy to care for must have a future.* I think this second thought too.

A bat flies past close to my head. Almost touching. What is the meaning of that? I shudder. I try to regain control of myself. I am so labile. My thoughts so volatile.

I see, coming from behind me, in the distance, the headlights of an approaching car. I cower. Yes, that also makes me scared. I'm scared of the dark, and I'm scared of lights. I feel around for the edge of the road, and then in the light of the approaching car, I see a shrub just big enough to hide behind. I lie down flat. Let the car go by. A factory van, taking a group of workers to start the night shift.

Why should I be scared of the lights of a van? Am I mad?

I want to stay here, hiding behind a shrub like a run-away. After swearing, lies, impersonation, receiving stolen goods, murder, now it's *being a runaway*. See how difficult it is to be a runaway. Even more difficult than being a slave? Freedom makes me scared.

I speak to myself: 'What should I do? I'm scared. I'm all alone. The world is a big place. It's dark everywhere. And dismal. The way is not lighted. I don't know the roads. I can't go forwards. Nor backwards. Nor stay put.'

Then I reply, loud and clear. 'Make a bit of headway, Krish, that's all. Get going! Move, now. Slowly but surely. To Montan Bol, turn left, go through Bosonz, past the litchi orchards, then you will find a place by the river to rest until morning. When the sun comes up, you can think what to do. You'll be in a good position then. OK? It's a positional battle, life is. Not just scoring goals!'

But it doesn't work.

I feel it coming. I start to cry. All alone. In the dark. Like a baby.

For the first time, I'm crying for his going. Tears follow tears. In that pitch dark.

I've lost him. *Lost. Friend.* It's over. He's gone. For ever.

At last, at long last, I cry.

Until I calm myself a bit.

The relief of it.

Was it that Captain, my new friend, made space in my heart for my sorrow for Baya? Captain, who reminded me that I'm not even eighteen yet? I'm *only* seventeen. That I can cry? That I am his little brother now. The little brother. Meaning I can cry for Baya now. There's Captain, and there's Kid. Anyone can cry. There's a time for crying. And a time for not crying.

And I start again, sitting down there, a big baby. And I cry out aloud. Huge tears, the size of a man's.

I suffer Baya's death *in my body*. It *speaks to my heart*.

119

I don't know how long I sit and cry like this. But when I'm exhausted, tired out, only then does the crying stop. Like a storm that shakes everything up. Then passes. And leaves a calm.

*

I get up and start to walk. One foot in front of the other again. Making headway.

Slowly, because of the darkness and my ignorance of the terrain. I keep at it, checking each footfall. Progress.

It isn't easy. And I am beginning to get hungry. I hadn't thought of that. Hunger. Thirst.

Swearing, lying, drinking, being handcuffed, a fugitive hiding in the woods. But I still haven't tasted sausage.

*

I go past the bright light at the stone-crusher's, get to Montan Bol, go on and cross the main road and turn left, meaning I start to go up towards Bosonz. Still the same slow way of proceeding. I face oncoming cars – there are strings of them – so they don't knock me over. Where are they all going? What business keeps them occupied all through the night like this? Some going up, others coming down. Agitation and useless movement. Fidgeting.

But I don't reach Bosonz, nor the litchi orchard, nor the Pyerfon roundabout. I'm dog-tired. Weak with exhaustion. Two days' fatigue spills over me. I'll find somewhere to doss down. I just want a bit of quiet, that's all, and a place to put my denim bag under my head and sleep a bit. I've been through too much. Results. The limousine. Flikanflak yesterday. Fishing. Sleeping on and off on the pirogue. The girl's body, her arms signalling to me. Arrested. And walking. Rest is all I want now. To repose my poor limbs. Peace and quiet and some internal music. Harmony. I want a deep new tranquillity, that's what I want.

And so I turn into a dirt road that wends its way into the sugar-cane fields on the side of the road. 'Maybe the Kaskavel road,' I think. I go in. I haven't got the foggiest what's waiting for me down that road.

But I start down it anyway. It is a rocky stretch of rough, uneven, untarred road. I make even less headway now. Then, when I guess I'm right in the middle of the sugar cane, in all that silence, on the edge of a path leading maybe to Kaskavel, I notice what seems to be a thick shadow on my left. Close by. I can feel its presence. Its vibrations. It must be one of those enormous piles of rocks. Do I recognize the smell of rocks? Does the pile of rocks have some personality it emits, from the time the rocks were piled up by slaves? I don't know. But I know it's here.

I go up to the pile of rocks, feel a boulder with my palms, hug it. I find a nice spot up against a huge old rock, and I curl up tight against it. I put my denim bag under my head, check that the bangle is still in there, protecting me, and prepare to go to sleep. An ideal place. Quiet. Sheltered from the night wind. Safe.

I check my trouser pocket. The thing is still there. I am still on my errand.

Sleep grabs me, pulls me in, and I give in and am gone.

*

I am standing on the roof of the Compagnie Nationale de Transport garage, and I am preparing myself psychologically for a grand effort. I am going to fly. I am captain of my own aeroplane, which is my body. I am going to jump off and fly. *This is your Captain speaking* I say. *We have lift-off.* My hands which are in handcuffs rise up in front of me. I shake my wrists and the handcuffs drop off. I put my arms out sideways like wide wings. I am wearing a broad shirt that has a hole in the middle of it that air will rush into to help with propulsion. With the concentration of an Olympic diver, I dive upwards, and then instead of falling down, I go on. I fly upwards and further upwards, the air rushing through the hole in my wide shirt. My legs are tied together with an orange ribbon, which is an advantage, because as a boy mermaid, I use them like a dolphin does when he swims, to assist my flying, and my legs are the tail of an aeroplane.

I am my own aeroplane. I lift upwards slowly but surely, against gravity, leaving the earth, and I need to keep my concentration so as to defy gravity, I need to use my arms and my legs. If I lose concentration, it is certain that I'll fall like a stone. Rules of the game.

I see a scene of unprecedented beauty, beyond imagination, below me.

The flower beds at the Bonnter nurseries. Thousands of flowers in heady colours, sunflowers at the back, and coral flowers tinkling with colour in the front, with marigolds to discourage the unwanted insects. Making a special effort, I manage to turn my head around even as I'm flying, and I see the sun coming out from behind the dark heavy mountain, as if it is throwing off a rug. It casts steel rays into the sky, rays that cut everything into geometrical segments, silver as blades. Each blade the blade of a giant fan that will protect our mother earth, as we protect her. There is joy everywhere, because each flower, as it buds, is raising its head to greet the sun, which pouts as it kisses each bloom. Everything is new and reborn.

Each ray gives light and colour to each petal, as if it were a clay lamp, lit by a match, each colour a love letter. Nirvana.

Coral blossoms raise their faces, zinnias in multitudes, and lettuce leaves rounding into folds, all tight in the middle, shy home-loving roses, mollycoddled, cover their thorns with pale shades of pink petal, Chinese lettuce bursts into leaf, gladioli grace the edges of vegetable gardens, and bringal trees produce leaves fiercely, forward anteriums show off for tourists, and when I, still flying, look very carefully, I see that there are two monkeys having a wedding under a chilli plant because it's raining while the sun is shining. The smell of perfume geraniums rises up to where I'm flying, and below me runner beans run amok, while thyme and parsley make a patchwork quilt of different greens, *so green you could swim in them*, and the strong smell of herbs overwhelms me. Crushed curry leaves. Allspice making me giddy with its perfect smell. And snakes of green rope that are the stems of pumpkin plants, heavy on the ground, the gourds ripe to bursting.

Each flower a face. Frank and open. Smiling. And their smiles, in the dream I know this, gradually become not just smiles, but laughs. And the laughter takes on a kind of rhythm, as if each voice were a musical instrument, and there is music now, and this music causes the beginning of a dance. But the dance is invisible because it is so beautiful.

When all of a sudden, a whole flock of birds that was in a frangipani tree goes on the wing, and the sound of their wings is like an orchestra of whish-whishing. *Wao wao, wao wao*. They beat their wings, and climb upwards until they come and meet me. The perfume of the frangipani so full so rich so sweet I could die. And they fly all around me, the konde with its red bottom, the yellow cape canaries each with a long fibre of coconut leaf in their beaks, little pingo birds, and swallows with clay in their beaks, some pairs of turtledoves with flying little ones, four or five parrots spreading loud rumours, one shrieking '*Boy!*' and a rush of pigeons from the bazaar, and a lone sandpiper, very busy. It cries out. Warning! Warning! *Avertisman! Tansyon!* Warning! We all fly together. And a bat comes so close to me, it touches me. And it whispers in my ear: 'It's time for bats to go to bed now. Replace me for the day shift, be a honey! I'm dead beat.'

I look down below and see the skeletons of vultured buses from the CNT in front of Jadoon's house. Like a graveyard. Waiting to be bought by CNT for spare parts. And I see Mauritius Telecom with a flag proud on its roof, and the hospital, the mortuary, bright and new, and through its window, yes the mortuary has a large sash window with a white lace curtain, billowing, blowing outwards in the breeze, and through its window come flying spirits, like seeds in the wind, representing the past. I know this representation. I go past above Lalwiz, the crossroads, and the bazaar, where a street merchant cries: 'I'm still here. Buy some *gato madelenge*, make the children happy.' From the CD shop, a sega blares out, '*Anita, mo gate*,' and hundreds and thousands of men and women and little children walk about as if in a dance. Really slowly and with grace. I see a beautiful young girl, with a lovely place just where her hair is blowing in the wind next to her neck, reminds me of seaweed moving under water, so I fly next to her, and lift her hair ever so lightly with my hand (her hair is light as a feather) and I whisper in her ear, 'Can I kiss you, just there, my sweetheart?'

She touches my neck.

*

A musk-rat scurries from under a rock in the pile, and in the hurry-hurry musk-rats are always in, it shrieks '*Chwink*', brushing against my neck. A second time it does this. This time it wakes me up. I shudder. I check with my hand that it hasn't bitten me. No. They sometimes bite, or so I've heard, and then they blow on the wound so you don't feel anything, then they bite again. So they say. And it bleeds.

But then, I lie dead still.

Because I become aware, gradually, of a sound, a very nearby sound: '*One two three four five six seven . . .*'

Fear rises in me.

Is it witchcraft? An incantation? I feel suspicion and more fear. I listen without moving a muscle. I look around me, but the darkness is thicker than ever. The sound is fearful. Treacherous. No matter how much I open my eyes wider and wider, I can't see anything at all.

What can it be? Who can it be? What ill luck brought me to lie down here, right near it? I'm still shuddering from the musk-rat, and now this sound. I shudder an even deeper shudder. The initial panic from the musk-rat doesn't subside, but only transforms itself into a worse panic. This hypnotic sound. The repetitions. The figures. The deep evil of it.

'What can such a sound *possibly* be?' I ask, trying to be more poised. 'Let me place myself. I'm near a pile of rocks in a cane field, maybe on the path to Kaskavel, when a musk-rat wakes me up to this sound. I am no longer on my own near this pile of rocks. What is going on?'

My beautiful dream over, I'm hurled into such disorder even before I can regret the passing of the dream.

I realize, even in all that fear that *that dream*, the girl's neck and all, was getting dangerous.

What if it had continued? I am horrified by the realization: *I haven't got spare trousers.*

My own body threatening to betray me like that.

Sublime to ridiculous, the words come to me. Internal things out of control, now *external* ones, musk-rats walking all over me. Disorder invading me.

I who know nothing.

The counting sounds get louder, pounding on my eardrums. The low voices more intent. Men's voices.

Oh my god.

I sweat fear. I don't move. Not an iota. I stop breathing. And as I begin to understand, I am seized by an even greater fear. Like an oil stain that goes on and on getting bigger, my fear spreads into my arms and hands and fingers.

'What's that?' I ask myself, 'Oh, my god!'

Some kind of black magic. Yes, a ritual of some kind. A system. A service. Getting rid of devils? Exorcism? Removing the evil eye?

Seems like the voices of three different men. Yes, three. And they are counting something. Counting and counting. Marbles.

'Don't be ridiculous,' I tell myself. 'Pull yourself together.'

I'm so frightened I could die.

'One, two, three, four, five, six, seven, eight, nine, ten.' They repeat this again and again. '*Enn de trwa kat senk sis set wit nef dis.*' Three voices. Auctioneers Cassette and Lasplaces, who sing out the bids in harmony.

'Must be money,' I think, 'Alibaba.'

I am more afraid.

Why exactly I am so scared, I don't know. I don't know *why*. But I know it's a good thing I'm scared. It's safer. It's more reasonable. It's essential.

'There you are! A thousand for you.' There is a kind of boss man who says this with authority.

His voice instills the worst fear into me. Cold and cruel, he is. Hard as nails. Merciless. Full of spite and senseless hatred. Generalized loathing for all in sight. Including me, no doubt.

Never knew how much a person can judge by just a voice. Never knew how much *I* could judge by just a voice. A voice in the pitch moonless darkness. One, two, three, just counting, no more than that. Chanting. Chanting. Chanting. And the one, their boss, some kind of soloist.

I know he could kill me in cold blood. Wring my neck. As if I were a Sunday chicken.

'*Kup liku kok, kup liku pul,*' the childhood refrain.

Tongue-tying, trip up and swear refrain. I put my hand to my neck, still smarting from the musk-rat brushing past like that, touching me. The refrain comes back, '*Kup liku pul, kup liku kok.*'

I see them cutting my head off. And, like a backyard chicken in Karo Lalyann when I was a child, I see my body running, running, running away even after my head is rolling in the dust.

Then the three men start again in chorus. Harmonics now. Devil harmonics.

'One, two three, four five six, seven eight nine ten.' When they get to ten, they raise their voices like children sitting on a primary school bench, learning to count. But these are clever, very clever, adults.

'There you are! A thousand for you now.' Again the voice of their boss. More harsh still this time round. He doesn't want to give them their thousand. The other two men are obedient. Scared of him. This is obvious, I hear it in their breathing which is fraught with agitation.

And there they go again, counting. 'One two three, four five six, seven eight nine . . . ten. That's three thousand rupees.' What are they doing with all this money, in the dark, in the middle of the cane fields next to a pile of rocks on a path that may lead to Kaskavel? I dread to think.

'There you are! Thousand for me. *For me.* Now count my second thousand.' Then he changes his voice, it gets even worse, '*Inn des trwas tire vu deor.*'

The boss gets two shares, the others each one. A share for the getaway car?

They count on and on. A thousand for this one, a thousand for that one, and two thousand for the boss. *Tire vu deor.*

I lie there without moving a finger. The arteries in my

neck are thumping loudly in my ears. The beating of a *ravann*. Warning me from afar. *Danger, Boy. Watch out, Boy. Danger, Boy. Watch out, Boy. Danger, Boy. Watch out, Boy.*

The palms of my hands sweat. Perspiration from my forehead runs down into my eyes, burning them. I stay still. I don't blink.

Suddenly, the fear is too much. I feel something hot inside my trousers. Oh, no, it can't be. I'm an adult. But it's true. I have let out a drop of piss into my pants. After Major pissing on my trousers, I'm now going to wet myself. And, like I've already said, I haven't got a change of trousers.

I concentrate on not letting any more pee come out. I ask myself: 'Didn't I tell you to go on through Bosonz? Now what! Didn't I tell you to go on down to the river? Stay right where you are now. Don't dare move, idiot, or you're in trouble. Big trouble.'

Don't I know it.

*

'And what in god's name is this! *Espes de kretin*! Excuse me!' His face is close to mine now. Bad breath.

'Gentlemen, we have before our eyes a fine specimen here, a new species?' I go cold.

He paces off. One of the assistants sneaks nearer. I feel a boot against my ribs, nudging.

He's going to kill me. I'm going to die.

Would they had kept me safe in the lock-up instead.

I know it. I'm in mortal danger. I am a witness. I am not dreaming. This is not a vision. Not a hallucination. It is happening. Raw and real. My life is in danger.

Here I note that a heavy dark cloud, it can't be anything else, has come and blotted out all the stars that were visible around the pile of rocks. There is a fine reflection on the edge of the cloud of the light of the stars, a flimsy *horni* on the cloud's shoulder.

That explains the heat. Clouds *do* that, they bring sudden waves of heat. I get time to think all these things.

And as the cloud gets thicker and bigger, everywhere gets darker still. And I get more and more terrified.

Not a star left now. No sign of the flimsy *horni* on the edge of the cloud. The cloud is everywhere now. You can feel it bearing down on everything. Heavy, heavy darkness. And heat.

'It's me,' is all I try to say, but my voice doesn't come out. I haven't got much breath left. 'It's me.'

'Well I never! That's *him*,' that same harsh voice spits this out with hatred. 'It is *he*. Good for you, then. Keep your mouth shut. Keep your eyes shut. Keep your fucking arsehole shut. Shut right up. *Espes de kretin*! No monkey business either! Shithead!'

The assistant nudges me with his boot a second time in the exact same place.

'Don't go and kill him,' the boss says. '*Espes de kretin.*' I've got a new name at last. At long last. With a *particule* in it and all. '*Espes de Kretin*! What the hell do you think you're doing here?'

Then he talks to the assistant. 'You're not *obliged* to do him in. If he should peg, it'll be *us* that's in deep water. Not him. He'll be fine. If it happens to be to our advantage to show pity to this *Espes de Kretin*, we will show pity, understand? Since when was pity a mortal sin? Pity can be an advantage.'

He stands above me, towering. I feel it. Then he puts something down next to my head. I smell kerosene. He strikes a match, and suddenly there is bright light from a hurricane lamp. I see a dirty cloth around its handle. He puts the lamp so near my face, I'm blinded. At least he isn't going to set me alight.

'Some kind of country bumpkin. What you seen then? Speak up! Your mouth sealed shut or something? Locked up with a padlock? The law of silence. Who do you work for then? Bye Kurupa? Talk, man! Or you dumb? *Espes de Kretin*! Or you've turned into a statue. On whose account are you working? Talk!'

With the bright light, I can't see anything. A bat in the daytime now.

'I live in the town. Vakwa.' I am too scared to start on lies now. But I don't want to own up to coming from Karo Lalyann. In case they laugh at me.

'What have you seen, then? No eyeballs in your head? No tongue in your mouth? No voice in your larynx?'

'Seen? I haven't seen a thing. What would I see anyway in this pitch darkness?'

'Hear? What did you hear, then? No jokes from you either, Smart Alec. One thing I can't stand is jerks who pretend to be jokers. Not in cane fields anyway. Not at midnight in the fucking pitch fucking dark. And not some kind of three-quarters of a person doing it either. Spare me.'

Before I have time to say anything, my ribs get nudged a third time. A final warning.

'No! Please! Save me!' My cries fly out into that silent night. But the cloud seems to blot up the sound. To eat it up. No chance of my cries reaching Kaskavel, if that's where we are near to. And even if anyone in Kaskavel woke up all of a sudden, hearing me, he would probably think someone was having nightmares and go back to sleep.

'Don't scare the kid. What did I tell you?' It's the boss again, speaking like a general who is sick and tired of his stupid lieutenants. 'How many times must I tell you. *Dead bodies are a nuisance.* Things that bring no advantage to us. They *port maler*. In our trade. We do hold-ups. We aren't common burglars. We are professionals. We are highwaymen. Robbers. We specialize. Do you understand me clearly? Code of ethics. And dead bodies is something we do not like. We do not need. They are superfluous. Hear me? Su-per-flu-ous.'

'But he isn't . . .'

'Chup-chap, you. Shut your trap.'

Then to me: 'Hear? What exactly did you hear?'

'Nothing, Sir, on my honour,' I manage to get out.

'No lies, if you don't mind. I can't stomach lies. What did you hear, stupid peasant!'

'I heard counting.'

'And what exactly do you think we were counting?'

'I don't know. I thought maybe you were counting marbles.'

The one who nudges my ribs, moves his boot towards my side. An ultimate warning.

'Tie him up. Arms and legs. And snout too. Gag him first, filthy dog! As if we haven't got enough on our hands, we have to get this joker, coming and pretending to be a big time storyteller. Already that watchman nearly killed me. Fucking hell. Counting marbles, indeed. Sitting counting marbles in the pitch dark. Could you just check if my shoulder's still bleeding? Bring the lamp over. Hurry up, or

I'll be leaving blood all over the place, and the dogs will get us all, and the forensic boys will identify it and all. Fucking watchman and his fucking gun.'

So the other man, the one who wasn't nudging me with his boot, goes over to him and shines a bright torch on to his right upper arm.

I see a filthy bandage around it. In the light of the torch. Blood dripping from it. He doesn't complain. Not one word. He just watches the blood dripping like that.

I take a look at this face.

Then I immediately regret it.

Not just the horrible expression on his face. Not just his demeanour. Not just the scar that slices his cheek in two, a scar that he might very well take out on me. Nor the one eye that grew back smaller than the other after it got burnt sometime in the past, maybe with acid, and that he could take out on me, too.

But what makes me regret having looked, is that the fact that I've seen his face might become good enough reason to kill me. He won't want a witness.

His assistants are being slow. They come and grab me, push a filthy cloth into my mouth, and tie my mouth up with a length of bandage. I am gagged. Then they tie my hands behind my back with coconut rope that cuts into my wrists. They tie my two feet together by tying my shoelaces together really tight. Baya's running shoes fettered. After so little running.

I should have worn sponge flip-flops.

Too late now.

When I try to complain, I can't even make much sound. I am silenced. Helplessness personified.

Then the dreaded words. The boss says: 'Search the little nosy-parker bastard, will you?'

No more than a touch on the spot, and the foot-nudger recognizes it. 'Bad boy! And what have we got here? What's it then? Answer me!'

He extracts the measure of gandya.

'I'll keep that, if you don't mind! Can you believe it? We honest men getting all ensnared with a little *drogé*? *Exhibit Number One, your honour.* Where's your base? A hanging crime now, you know! Or forty-five years inside if you're lucky. No bail, nothing. Or should we just hand him over to those nice policemen down in Banbu? They say they don't *caress* their detainees there.'

He is so pleased. 'Don't give them a cup of tea, they say. The forces of law and order are interested in this kind of offence these days. Very interested. As it is, the magistrates are clamping down. *There is too much of this sort of thing going on*, they say. Hardly out of the cradle and into cannabis. Where will this lead the country?'

Failed, I think. I have failed. My errand not done. Not run. My mother asked only that of me. A mission, she said, and I corrected her. Go and run an errand. Fetch a commission. Uncle Dip said 'Careful', and I haven't been.

I have *failed*.

'Wait,' the boss says, full of pompous lessons to his assistants. 'This is the exact kind of young man we have to be *very* careful of. Can't just leave him *here* either. Out of the question. Shit! We've got to get rid of him. No doubt one of those sneaky little criminal types, playing dumb, pretending he was born yesterday. Yeah, let's take him some place else. Undo the legs. You two walk on the outside, give him the middle.'

They snuff the lamp out. And the boss instructs them to switch off the torch. And we walk slowly in that ink-darkness, each of them touching an arm to check I'm still there. To their car. My mouth is already uncomfortable, making me gag. That's why they call it *gagging* you. I manage to think this.

Yes, they've got a car. They switch on the torch, so I see it. It's a smart hire car, parked just inside the cane fields, hidden from the main road. Blue-green, the colour of a parrotfish. And as shiny. A taxi number. Probably false number plates, I find myself thinking.

'Close his fucking eyes, then, what are you waiting for, for him to see us all?' the boss spits out orders. 'In passing headlights, he'll see us clear as day. *A little knowledge is a dangerous thing.* Better he doesn't know anything at all.'

Now it's the darkest dark. My eyes are bound tightly behind a thick band. Not even different shades of darkness now. Only imaginary colours sparked off by my brain, video clips, with spots moving outwards. Fireworks. Black background and spider webs of colours knitted in circles. Shining and shimmering at the edges. Little lines of yellow follow one another from left to right in my vision, passing fireflies.

They shove me into the car.

'We'll unload this some place.' I know he's talking about me. Unload me. 'Then we bring the car back, leave it right here, as we planned it. We must *follow our plan*. An important principle, learn it, men! Don't let this little runt disturb our well-made plans.'

I get more frightened. Unload me. Over a cliff? Into the sea? My only hope is the fact that the boss doesn't like corpses. But if they load me over a cliff into the sea, he won't have one. Unless I wash up somewhere.

Some hope.

They push my head down on the back seat between the two of them, the two assistants. Then they lean heavy elbows on my back.

And with that, the car sets off. The boss at the wheel despite his injury. They go round and round a bit on the spot. Confusing me. Then he puts his foot down, and we're off. I don't know how long this lasts. Bends in the road. Endless. I hear the sea at one point. The reef, very loudly. I get a whiff of sea air somewhere else. Low tide. Some rotting seaweed. Then inland for a long time. Then we go right down, it seems, towards a river, I hear the car crossing a bridge, then the car goes up again, then down again, another bridge. Then a third bridge. I can't work out where I am. I am dizzy.

Slowly, I say it to myself, 'They're kidnapping you, Krish. Oh, boy!'

It starts to rain now. I smell it. And I hear it under the wheels.

I can't remember the list of my offences. From lies and swearing, to murder and drugs, now I'll be accused of doing whatever it is these men are doing?

And then they stop the car.

They push me out.

There's rain falling on my forehead. The kind of silent rain that is like very thick fog. A chill rain. Maybe it's Nuvel Frans, or Klini, or god knows what hellhole. I don't know those wetlands very well. My dad's father's family are from Banann. Always raining there.

Behind me, the engine is switched off. The two assistants come around to me, pull me up and frogmarch me. Blindfolded, I stumble between them. The coconut rope cuts into my wrists. The ground underfoot is uneven and soft. A tin door squeaks open. Sound effect of a late-night horror film.

They push my head down, and then shove me hard into what I think is a shed. *Unloading* me. Getting rid of me.

Straw underneath me. Smells good. And for a split second, I feel a kind of pleasure. The softness of being put to bed very, very tired. Climbing back into my mother's womb. Maybe with a second chance to be born. This time not a breech.

Then I jerk myself to my wits.

I've got to work out where I am. A makeshift hut of some kind? An old abandoned house? An animal shed? But there is no smell of cows or goats here. There is the smell of straw. A rich, grilled smell. Food has been cooked near here. I get the distinct smell of an open hearth. *Sunndur*. Roasted rice. But as for where I am, I just don't know.

Will they just leave me here on my own? Trussed up like a chicken? To die?

Then they start saying goodbye to me.

'Good luck, you stupid little nuisance, half-baked little devil. Heads you don't live, tails you die,' says the voice of the man who nudges. Then he laughs. '*Pe badine, do.*'

Then two of them walk away. I hear them. Squelch, squelch.

The boss speaks now: 'You keep this, keep your filthy drugs. And keep your silence too, hear? Unnerstann? That is the contract. You say anything, we get you with an *allegation*. We set you up for drugs.'

I try to make a sound like 'I agree'. He pushes the *puliah* of gandya back into my trouser pocket. Where it came from. Then he slaps me on my hip, playfully.

And adds: 'And a couple of rupees for the road. *For your silence*. Honesty among thieves. If you die, you die. If you live, these rupees may pay your way. *In silence*. You talk, we get you done for drugs.'

He squeezes a whole roll of money, I can't tell how much, into my other trouser pocket. To him, it's nothing.

My denim bag, I remember it. It's gone. My pillow near the pile of rocks in Kaskavel lies there still.

If I live, I've got problems. If.

Then he puts his face close to mine, breathes on my neck, and puts something cold to it. A gun? A knife? A car ashtray? I am too scared to tell the difference.

And he is off.

I am on my own now.

I hear his footsteps fade away. Back down the path. Car doors bang closed, the engine kicks up, and roars off.

Quietness all around me now. The sound of the car starts to trail off.

Good riddance.

Relief that they are gone. Where am I, and what am I going to do? I can't hear any sounds now. Just the car moving further and further away.

They forgot to tie my feet up again. Small mercy. But the coconut rope chafes my wrists, my eyes are still tightly blindfolded and my mouth still gagged.

And I feel *relieved*.

I've got my errand back again. I haven't failed in running an errand for my mother. Not yet, anyway.

*

How am I going to get out of here? Will I die? I don't seem to want to die any more. Just when I can die without much effort.

I'm in deep trouble. Up to the neck.

Worse trouble than ever before. These robbers and

highwaymen, whatever they are, are heading back for Kaskavel. They are going to leave their car there. There will be clues.

And my very own denim bag will be right there. Baya's bangle in it. With his name inscribed on it. And there is even a policeman in Banbu who will recognize the bag at once. And the bangle. Fucking hell. On the scene of the crime. Blood of the boss nearby. Proof against me. I did the hold-up. Evidence.

And then. What if I get Captain and Kid into trouble too?

Oh my god.

My mouth is tied up, so I can't even talk to myself properly. But I laugh at myself, murmuring: 'Now you're up shit creek, Krish.'

'No need to rub it in,' I reply to myself.

Tied up, hurled into a stable, given up for dead.

I give a smothered wail, a gagged sob. Not for my own death, but for *why did he have to die?*

Pure sorrow now.

As I am crying like that, like a baby, it comes to me even stronger that I want to survive. I am going to live.

I cry for Baya's life. So short. His slow smile gone for ever. I won't be able to tell him, not ever, about what's happening to me now. He isn't here to guide me any more. He'll never write another poem for me. Nor tell me a single new story.

I cry for hours. So it seems.

Then, here in this hut, this stable, a new peace comes to me. The sound of a fine drizzle on the tin door. The rope cutting into my wrists doesn't matter. Nor does it matter that my mouth is tied so tight I can hardly swallow.

I've made peace with my Baya. *I love him.*

Everything always in movement. Shifting. Changing. Alive, living. Raw with change.

I want to pee, for example.

I crawl around the edge to the door and stand up, leaning against it.

What am I going to do, hands tied up, how will I even open my flies? *Save me!* I don't want to pee in my pants again. I try to undo my hands, but the coconut rope is rough and unrepenting.

So I rub my jeans against the doorpost and succeed in getting the button to pop open. Luckily no belt. I pull at my pants from behind with my clumsy thumbs. And the zip gives and starts to come down. I get my pants down far enough, then my underpants. Not easy. I try the door. It doesn't open and I'm too tired. So I move over to the corner, for privacy, and I succeed in peeing into that corner. Kneeling down. Like I was saying a prayer.

But I hadn't thought of how to get my jeans back on again. That turns out to be a long struggle. I get them more or less up, but there's nothing to be done about the zip and the button.

'Bad luck,' I tell myself.

But I stay worried. Even when I'm lying there. In case my trousers fall down. It is useful, sometimes, to have a practical concern.

Let me go to sleep, then, will you?

And so, for the second time in the very same night, I fall into a deep, deep sleep.

*

I wake up in a sudden panic-stricken state. A child scared in the night. *Where is my Baya?* Then pain all over me. Every inch of me is sore. And I become aware of *dread*, a dread of what might come to pass.

Come to pass.

I want to breathe through my mouth. Urgently.

And I begin to worry. What if? What if I want to get sick? To vomit? What if my nose gets blocked? What if? I put all my effort into *not panicking*.

Calm yourself, I mutter into the gag.

And then I hear a sound. The distinct sound of a car approaching. Fear and relief mingle in me.

Friends arriving to save me? Enemies to harm me? Indifferent people who will shrug and leave me pretending they didn't even notice me?

And how to tell the difference?

I've lost the door.

I crawl around, fall around, and find it. Only to re-member it's latched.

I'll have to open it with my feet. I brace myself against all pain and discomfort. These are only sensations, I convince myself. So, I lie down opposite the closed door on my back, crushing my burning wrists, put my feet up against it, and push. With all my might. But it doesn't move. I stand up and then, back at the door, grope around, my pair of tied-together hands one useless limb. A loop of rope that I recognize. It's one of those funny loops people put on the inside of doors, so that you can only open and close them from the outside by putting your hand through a hole in the door itself.

Luck is with me. *Ha! Ha!* And with this thought I remember Baya's bangle. My good luck charm. And flooding back comes the memory of my bag lying next to a pile of rocks, incriminating me. In god knows what.

I tell myself, *let the pain flow over me*. And it does.

I crawl out the door on my knees. It's drizzling. I try and scream. 'Mmum, gmugmmu,' I manage to get out, 'Ngnnng.'

And I stand up and start walking.

This is when I overhear two voices. Low and slow and kind.

Are they from inside the car?

I stop and listen. Better safe than.

Honey-smooth jocular men's voices floating out into that drizzle. I listen. Now some jazz music starts up, low behind their voices. A laconic singer.

I could cry with happiness.

The first man's voice quiet, teasing, says, 'And what the hell time did you come wake me up then, Vasenn? What if it's only two o'clock, and we're sitting here waiting?'

A warm silence. The jazz music is blues. So gentle I could weep. One of them's called Vasenn.

'It's still pitch dark, man.' I can hear in his voice he's laughing at himself.

There's another long gap. The music warms to a mellow rhythm, the voice now sings: '*Easy come, easy go*'.

'I just woke up in a panic, with that *feeling* that I'd overslept. And worried. What if you *shouted* at me for being late again!' – here they both laugh loudly, and listen to the music for a long time, for what seems like ages – 'I got up so fast, got dressed so quick I didn't even put my underpants on.' More laughter. 'Just knew "I've got to wake Vikas up. In case he swears at me for oversleeping."' The other one is called Vikas.

'And in case we don't get today back again if we miss it. Gone for ever. A lost chance.

'But, come to think of it, the banana vans weren't out yet.'
This sets them off laughing again.
'And here we are out with strike leaflets.'
Strike leaflets, I'm in a *strike*, now.
Oh, my god. My father says the trouble with this country is the strikes.
More silence. An acoustic guitar takes up the pattern of the singing voice. In that drizzle.
They talk slow and lazy, long, intimate gaps between.
'Not *strike leaflets*, Vasenn. Remember?' Yes, Vasenn must be younger. 'We are here with *no strike leaflets*!'
Vasenn laughs a belly laugh.
More music. More ease.
What are they talking about? *No strike*. Laughing about?
I never heard anything like it. They are so close.
Me and Baya were, too.
'Especially Rozbel,' one says, and this makes them laugh more.
So we are in the Rozbel Estate area.
Vasenn answers now, 'I can see fuck all. Light a match for me, Vikas, do a guy a favour. Throw light on the matter.'
I hear him throwing the box of matches. And I hear my father saying '*that* will bring *the ruin of the country*'. Not smoking. *Strikes*.
Suddenly, loud swearing: 'Stop it! What you doing to me! Let me sleep a bit more!' The third voice now. Cursing, groggy, complaining, sleepy. 'What's the matter with you guys?'
'Quick! Put it out!' Vasenn's voice calls out in sudden panic, 'Vikas sets your hair on fire, and you complain when I put it out!' Laughter that then subsides.

143

More quiet. And the music calm in that heavy drizzly quiet.

The hauntingly beautiful music rises in the silence. I edge closer, pulling my trousers up all the time.

'What the bloody hell!' Vasenn now, and he starts laughing again. 'It's half past bloody three in the bloody morning, idiots!' More laughter.

Silence.

It's then that my knee hits something with a *bang*. I could die of shock. The flank of the car itself. I slump down on the spot in a pool of fear.

'What was that?'

'Watch out!'

So I try to call out again.

'Mmum, gmugmmu,' I say, 'Ngnnnng.'

When Vasenn, I guess it's him, opens his car door, he strikes a match right next to my face. I hear it, I smell it.

I don't know whether to be terrified now. Or relieved. So I just sit there, seized up.

'Hey, what you think you're doing? Oh my god, come and have a look at this. Oh my god. It's a kid with his mouth gagged. And his eyes blindfolded. And his flies are undone, and his trousers are coming down. Just by the car. Come and look. Hurry. And they've tied his hands up behind his back.'

I hear another car door opening. It's a *radio play*. I've fallen into a radio play?

'What have they gone and done to you. Poor kid,' in the voice you speak to babies in. I'm back to being a baby now. Not just Boy. 'In no time we'll free you, won't we? There you are. Is that better?' As though he is changing my nappy.

'Undo his hands, Vasenn,' Vikas says. 'It's only a kid.'

'A young man, it is,' Vasenn says.

I've passed the test at last. *A young man.*

*

And with that, it starts raining hard, pouring down. One of them switches the headlights on, one unblindfolds me. And through curtains of rain I make out the thick creepers all around us, layered forever, an abundance of heart-shaped leaves covering all the shrubs. Undergrowth riotous, lush, thick. Leaves of red and green. Long thin ones, red and yellow. Tall elephant grass. Mossy bark and ferns. An orchid growing on the bark of a tree. Then the headlights are off again.

Vikas, now undoing my hands, says in a monologue, as if to himself: 'Curse this Rozbel rain. Push your feet into wet boots in the morning, walk to work in the rain, work in the cane in the rain, and then when you're finished, walk home in the rain. Fucking hell.'

He shoves me into the car. Ah, the warmth, the softness. I could just curl up now and sleep with my new family.

An old Toyota Corolla or something. Clapped out.

'Don't want trouble. We've got work on our hands.' Only then does he undo the gag from my mouth.

'My head's sore,' I start. Vikas lights another match. I see him angular and thin. I see laughing eyes, even in that dark. Now, Vasenn darker and rounder. Toni sitting in the front passenger seat, next to Vasenn. Fast asleep. Cherub. Locks of curly hair on the top of the headrest. I can see how those caught fire. Then the match goes out.

145

They start the questions. *I am so tired.*

What to tell them? I am dog-tired. My tongue bruised, I stutter out a version: 'Waiting for a bus in Montayn Long when a car offers me a lift, I get in. Men in the car attack me, tie me up and bring me here, lock me up in hut. Why? I dunno.'

New lies.

'Why?' Vasenn asks me.

'Why?' I reply, 'How would I know why? They think I'm a witness to something they did.'

I spin out anything now.

'Rather fishy little story of yours,' Vikas chips in. 'Rather fishy.' Can't get anything past Vikas.

'Most unlikely,' Vasenn adds. 'What's your name, then?'

'Krish.'

'Krish who?'

'Burton.'

'Where do you live?' Vasenn, like in a court case on TV. Counsel for the prosecution.

'Karo Lalyann.' I study them now. Vikas listening, the whites of his eyes so piercing I know he knows when I'm telling lies.

'What work you do?' the counsel for the prosecution continues.

'I don't work.'

'Unemployed?'

'Only just left college.'

He turns around in his seat and asks Vikas to light another match. He checks my cut wrists.

'Story's a bit threadbare, that's all.'

Let me just curl up right here and sleep. Let me just.

And at this very moment, I whisper to myself: 'Ask

them, go on, ask. Don't miss your chance, now. Ask them outright! Now's your chance!'

So I come out with it: 'Can I stay with you for today, please?'

'Today? Stay with us today? Of all days!' Vikas whistles loudly next to me, and pulls his cap over his eyes.

'Age?'

'Eighteen.' I'm used to this particular lie now.

'Drive?' still Vasenn talking. They need a driver maybe.

'Yes.'

But I tell them I haven't got a licence yet.

'How come you can drive, then?'

'My dad's a taxi driver.'

'What you think then, Vikas? Can he stay with us?'

The car seat moves. Vikas is shrugging. It means 'yes'. Relief comes over me. I begin to shiver, even in the warmth of the car. Fear passing. Leaving me shivering.

'We've got the whole of the south and the west to do. So don't make a nuisance of yourself, got it? That's a condition.'

Oh my god, the whole of the south and the west to do. I'll do anything.

My father warned me against unions. *They stir things up.*

I never heard such things before. My head dizzies as they talk.

'Got this merry-go-round strike coming up. Got to break this false boss's strike *first*. All around the whole country, small teams, like this, ruining *their* supposed strike.'

Then I begin to pick up only phrases. I'm too tired now. *Delegates decided. Merry-go-round tough to organize. Get wind of false strike call. Delegates meet again. Block*

*it. Government in cahoots. Work conditions so bad work-
ers may come out on false strike. Bosses know this. If false
strike succeeds, problems, problems. The new law.*

'All this to say,' he goes on, 'that we haven't got time to
look after a stupid little baby today.'

A *little* baby now. It's true, back from *Boy* to *baby*. I feel
faint.

'My father said . . .'

'*My father.* Your arse. Fucking taxi drivers, what did I
tell you Vasenn? Shit in their heads. Your father own a
fucking sugar estate?' Silence, as this sinks in.

Silence. Even the music has stopped.

'I'm thirsty,' I say. Vasenn passes me a bottle of water.

The warmth of no one speaking. Letting their words
sink in, meanings taking root.

'Vikas here, labourers' union, Krish. A labourer. Me,
mill workers' union, an electrician. This sleeping hulk,
unemployed.

'We are in charge of sugar and salt,' he says. 'Leaflets
before the sun comes up today. And site visits all day long.
See?

'There's tea in the thermos. Drink it down. Here, two
paracetamols. Down them too, for the pain.' As I tilt my
arm to pour the tea into the thermos lid, pain shoots up to
my shoulder, but I manage. I put that sweet milky vanilla
tea to my lips and feel a warm contentment and happiness
infuse my whole body.

They turn the tape over. More mood music. Slow jazz.

My bruised tongue comes back to life.

Out of the blue, Vikas asks: 'No weapons on you? No
pen knife? Nothing?'

'No, why?'

'Because we ask, that's why.'

148

'Nothing else? Stolen goods, marihuana?'

Silence.

More silence.

I've been found out.

'What the hell,' Vikas sighs, 'What have we gone and landed ourselves with now?

'Bodysearch him, Vasenn. Something's up. Causing us a lot of shit, this one. Cut the sentimentality about him. Easy come, easy go.'

He sings these last words from the song. *Easy come, easy go.* I see a hardness in them that frightens me now.

I tell them. A *puliah* in my pocket.

'Use the stuff?'

Mother sent me to my Mamu in Krevker. For Maha-shivratree. Bhang for services. Please don't kick me out.

'Spare us your stupid stories!' Vikas sighs, 'Lucky we bloody checked. Give me it, Vasenn. A fucking little *puliah* of fucking gandya. Drugs charge, that's what we need. Set us up for *dealing.*'

He puts his head back and roars with laughter: 'I see it already. *Faits divers* column: *Des drogués notoires font trépass sur la propriété sucrière de M. X: arrestations juste à temps.* Wouldn't even need to fight out the *real strike, false strike* question.'

With that Vikas just takes the gandya, opens his door, gets out and takes one almighty swing and throws the *puliah* of gandya as far from the car as he can.

My mother's errand.

Into the darkness in Rozbel. Into a curtain of knotted bushes weeds shrubs creepers, a thatch of growth, a fury of different greens.

Vikas curses my mother and uncle. 'See? Hypocrites. They the fuckers that say hang people for drugs. True?'

'Mmm,' I say.

I realize, with horror, I'm falling. Falling. I see the hypocrisy I have only vaguely smelt.

Seeing it makes me feel dizzy, falling, dizzy.

My mum at that neighbourhood meeting, where they call in the police commissioner, be hard on youth. On substance abuse, she starts to call it. *Substance abuse* meeting. Clamp down, they said. On who?

Dizziness.

On people like herself? *I'm falling.*

Sending me. *I feel faint.*

I fall into silence. Wait for my head to steady.

Silence.

I help myself to another lid-full of sweet milky vanilla-flavoured tea.

And sink into the music. Low-key music. They say it's a Kirpip group, special for its mixture of jazz, blues, sega, country and western.

Happiness infuses me. Like tea brewing.

A word game. I've never played this. Words and ideas thrown into the air, for the pleasure of it, and for the outcome.

Vasenn asks if it's true I've just finished school. Or lies. I say *true.*

'Well, where you going to work, then?'

I'll just look for a job, I say.

'You look for a *boss.*'

I begin to laugh. 'I'll be looking for a *person*, you think?'

'Who knows?' he answers.

Toni the Storyteller, with the funky music in the background, starts to tell stories as he wakes up. Slow stories. Stories about the police and prisons, about stingy bosses and strike-breaking workers, about scabs and heroes, about errors and omissions, about losing face in front of overseers, about meetings where the speaker loses his voice, stories of victories and of defeats, of heroism and cowardice, old stories, new stories, borrowed stories, blue stories, night stories and day-time stories.

All true stories.

Stories that are happening all around me, and I don't even know it.

The day the public address system started squeaking at the very peak of a public meeting when Vasenn was addressing a huge crowd, and Toni thought it *was* the sound system. But it was Vasenn's throat. And how Vikas thought Vasenn would *croak*. The day the goats crossed over between orators and crowds just as Vikas took the mike. The day the other speakers didn't turn up and Vikas had to go on and on, always restarting with 'Another important point, *mo bann kamarad* . . .' The day the . . .

Soothing stories. Like they're all healing me.

I nod off to sleep.

Until the very first bit of daylight comes into the sky. Hardly perceptible, making the cane leaves down the road stand out pointed and black against the pale sky, contrasting with the thick rounded leaves of the forest we are in.

We get out, spruce ourselves up. Vikas gets a brush out of the car somewhere, and tries to brush my clothes down. My T-shirt's still caked in mud. He tilts his head to one side, then goes and gets out a beautiful bright-green, hand-knitted pullover, with white patterns knitted into it, across the chest.

They nod in admiration when I pull it on. Vikas comes and pulls it straight, patting it into place. My jeans are still terrible, but no one will notice them now. They'll only see the white pattern on that green pullover. Toni combs my hair.

'Here's your pile of leaflets, Krish.'

I didn't dream they would let me help.

'You hold the pile like this. Respecting, in your gestures. The *oldest* person may be the next one to take a leaflet from you. Yes, that's right now, Krish.'

My name. He uses my name.

'Each time, you concentrate on that one person. Focus all your attention. You are giving *him* one. You are giving *her* one.'

Like teaching me to dance.

*

I would never have dreamt it. In no more than three minutes from just that first hint of lightness in the morning sky, in the middle of that Rozbel fog, on a road no more than a dirt track joining a bit of woodland forest, thick with creepers and lush with undergrowth, to the first Rozbel cane fields, I find myself somewhere that becomes a busy crossroads. *Springs to life.* First a man on a bicycle goes past, takes a leaflet without stopping. *He has done this before, he is used to it.* Not a speaking kind of man. Then a group comes by, each one says good morning, and still walking on, takes a leaflet. They have also done this before, right here. Then in a warm hubbub of talk, a large group of women labourers come up to us, and stop. One has her hoe over her shoulder, no hands. Another two have theirs on their heads pointing forwards, and three have theirs on their heads pointing backwards. The rest have their hoes balanced diagonally across their heads. All, no hands. They wear blue plastic bagging on their shoulders and around their waists, like aprons. For the rain. They stand in interested silence, in their gumboots, waiting. I watch the others. They wait. Then one woman, who must be nearing retiring age, speaks.

'Will you tell us about this, son?' she says, 'Explain to us?' Each one has a different kind of hat on her head, under the hoe. They wait.

And this is my first trade union meeting. No chairs. No chairperson. No minutes. Nothing. Question and answer. *That's why they are so good at it*, I think to myself, *they get practice*. The tones of quiet intimacy. Love. This is shocking to me. I reel under lost prejudice, I never would have dreamt. I pick up the caring atmosphere. Most often I hear the sounds from the women or from Vikas, depending on who's talking and who's listening: 'Oh! Oh, mm. Mm. Yes. Mm. Ah.' Then more question and answer. Call and response. A song. Doubt expressed, reassurance given. A quiet urgency in the air. Birdsong. I hear things I have never heard of, a whole new world, a new vocabulary, 'the draft agreement', 'labour law suspended', 'won't keep 18% of workers in intercrop any more', 'the 1964 card system is threatened', 'convert new workers into seasonal like indenture', 'slavery returning'. I understand nothing. An ignoramus. A handicap to Vasenn, Vikas and Toni.

And I feel quite faint as I realize that behind every cane field, so invisible to me as I lie asleep in my mother's house, as I go about in my father's taxi, all over the whole country, in the mornings, even as in the day, and this has gone on for two hundred years, there are workers going to work like this, and I don't know it. Me sleeping away. I, a colonizer of my own land. I am giddy at my own ignorance, my own internal emptiness. And to imagine that the distribution of leaflets, like this one, is going on right now all over the country. I can't believe it.

I warm under the privilege *to be* here.

To be part of something.

Something that may mean something.

Something that may change something.

I learn.

By chance, I learn. I am finding out. By a quirk of destiny. To think I could have wasted my whole life missing this reality! Vasenn knows about it. Vikas knows. Even Toni knows. Because they are here. They listen, they look and they learn.

One woman labourer asks Vasenn for eleven leaflets. Now that she understands. Another woman takes fourteen because she will be in Klini this afternoon. Another needs ten or so to take to Rivyer Dipos tomorrow morning. Another is a member of the Co-op shop, needs twelve for other members who will be at an assembly. And the last asks for fifty, because she will go to Gro Biyo in person this afternoon, and hand them out. *They* often get left out, she says, and then they make mistakes and then people blame them, they say, 'Oh, the Gro Biyo lot fucked it all up again.'

This is how it goes on.

I am bewitched.

It is magic.

And as the numbers die down to just the odd cyclist, I am sad it's all drawing to a close.

'Is that all?' I ask.

'Now we're off to the mill gates. That's easier. We'll meet the other groups giving out leaflets there, too.'

But it isn't all.

Suddenly, there's a bicycle coming towards us fast. Words of warning. Quickly delivered.

'Police!' he cries, pointing to where we should go and pedalling like mad, 'Turn round and follow!'

We pile into the Toyota in two seconds, and doors still closing, Vasenn whips the car round in the mud, accelerator roaring, and we skid off down the alley-road after the high-speed bicycle.

I look around. Blue light flashing. Oh my god. The police are after us. What have I done now?

Vasenn accelerates over a steep blind rise, and down after the lightning bicycle. It turns sharply off the road to the left, while the road itself veers to the right.

On after him. Suddenly we are lost in a quiet slip road and have turned 180 degrees. He signals us to cut the engine and stop, hidden behind a thick barrage of green trees and shrubs and creepers.

Silence.

The police car tears past us, over the blind rise, and curves off to the right, following the road.

The cyclist just signals us on back to where we came from, meaning no hurry now.

'Take them a while to find anywhere to turn round,' Vikas says.

My heart is beating wildly. At least I haven't got my errand in my jeans pocket any more.

We all start singing *easy come, easy go*.

And so it's in music that we head for the mill. Too many people there for the police to get up to any hanky-panky, Vasenn says.

What would the police have done to us? If we hadn't been warned by the man on the bicycle.

On to the mill.

There, mill workers, irrigation men, garage mechanics, stop their bicycles one by one, cut their motorcycle engines, put a foot down on the ground, share a few words. They are hungry for details. For arguments. Easy to spread word here. Only one gate. While labourers criss-cross the entire countryside on foot, on bicycles, in lorries, and work in gangs of twenty. So Vikas tells me.

I remember how my Mamu Dip and my mother 'send word' to one another. Which brings me to hoping Mamu hasn't got word through to her that I've left their place.

By five past seven all the mill workers have gone in. It is quiet outside the gates now. Still.

Our next rendezvous is with the eleven others who have been distributing leaflets in cane fields in the Rozbel Estate area. It's at a snack bar in the centre of the village.

'Fourteen *roz tyed*,' Vikas says, 'and one *sanpayn*.' Never heard these words. Tea with milk, poured from a dizzy height into the mug, fourteen. And black tea, one. We each eat a hot *makacha*, the coconut and butter melting into it. One big table. Bubbling with stories, laughs, plans. *Makacha* dipped into sweet fizzy tea.

Then the four of us separate off again and head for the Risano sugar estate. A patchwork country of sugar estates I had never seen.

As we get there, we train our eyes into the distance. Against the green sugar-cane plants, against the rolling fields, we look for teams of labourers. Then we stop at a distance, get out and wait. We wait.

When they recognize Vikas, they drift to the edges of the field near us and take leaflets. Share words with him. The sirdar looking on, surly. Resentful, outnumbered.

'Not one toe on the boss's field though, Krish. Or it's the *kolom*'s shotgun.'

I can't even see a *kolom*.

Risano, at the mill, Vasenn walks in, leaflets under his shirt, arms swinging. He climbs up to his friend who works way up on the derrick. Slips him the leaflets. In his tea break, the friend will circulate them. In the mill, in the garage, to all the drivers as they come in. He knows how to do this.

At eleven sharp we drive in to the Leskalye Village Hall. And this is when I get to be at my first *big* meeting. Ahuja loudspeakers and all. I see now. *Sharing a common understanding.* Women in gumboots and navy-blue uniforms, wide-brimmed hats against the midday sun, their task work finished, exhaustion on their faces. The men, hoes on their shoulders, ashen with the physical work of the day finished.

Everyone's faces lit up with plans.

Foiling *their* plans, building *ours*.

Then to Britannia, this time to the tied housing. There, old ladies, young women and girls, mothers, wives and daughters come out, winding their *hornis* around their waists. A different kind of meeting. Low-key. Background information. Whispers and suggestions. If the women understand, the menfolk give them the respect due to them. So Vikas says.

All this I did not know.

Someone bursts in, panting, warns us. The boss has done a round, seen us. Then we look up and see a riot police vehicle winding down a road in the distance. We are on tied housing.

Again, we slip away.

Then off to distribute leaflets and have smaller meetings

at Sent Oben, Linyon Dikre, Belom estates. I realize it is not that we are distributing leaflets so much as talking and listening around the leaflets.

'Belom,' Vikas says, 'is where convicts transported from India nearly two hundred years ago had a rebellion.' The past moves into the present as we go along.

To the salt pans now. Rush, rush, rush. Before the workers go home for the night.

There's lots of salt because of the drought on the west coast, so they are working until six.

At Ti Rivyer Nwar the flat pans are all around us. As far as you can see. They're built of hewn basalt rock, in perfect squares, with shallow seawater slowly crystallizing into salt. White against the black hewn rock. Here raked into piles. Here already in baskets. Here even in bags. Here piled up in mountains, waiting for lorries to cart them off. A narrow road, no more than two tracks for the tyres, sliced between the hewn salt pans.

It is more than a mile long.

Vasenn drives in tentatively. Looking left, looking right. The bosses here shoot, he says. On sight.

No sign of any boss. No sign of any boss's car.

But, just as we get near the shed where the workers are gathered, something comes into sight.

'Oh, my god,' sighs Vikas, and I hear real consternation. There's a car parked there.

'What's the boss doing here?' Vasenn says, slamming the car into reverse, turning his head right round, and speeding backwards.

Within seconds, the boss's car is after us. Forwards.

But we've got an advance.

The sound of high revs in my ears, and so excited I could die, a mile in reverse.

We make it to the main road, Vasenn quickly gets into first, second and off at high speed, back where we came from.

'Industrial relations in salt are hot,' Vikas explains, 'But once we're off his property, he won't shoot. He won't do anything.'

Third chase in one day.

So we go back to the Ti Rivyer Nwar village and look for someone trustworthy to leave the leaflets with. Just a few, Vasenn explains, because only one or two can read. A delegate is home on sick leave for the day. '*Vey lanbeli.* With our boss, you always have to wait for the moment of the calm spell.' Then he repeats it, *wait for the moment of the calm spell.* 'Leave a few more,' he explains, 'their children read them to them.'

'Home?' says Vasenn.

So we set off home.

I don't know where home is. I'm too tired to ask. Vasenn says don't worry, his is near mine.

*

'Eat up then, Krish,' Vasenn's wife says, 'He told me to look after you. What happened to you then, you look a wreck? Though that green pullover is . . . well, stunning.'

'Vikas lent it to me. Oh, lots of things happened to me,' I say, 'All sorts of things. Good and bad.'

'Leave him alone,' Vasenn says to her, 'He can tell you another time.'

'Another time! *Hmm!* Another time. You always tell me

that. I'll be asleep later when you guys get back and I'll still be asleep when you get up in the morning, that's what.'

She serves us at table. Pumpkin-leaf soup, all green with a ginger taste slightly stronger than the garlic taste, new potatoes the size of marbles, curried dry in their jackets, a fish rogay, bright red with tomatoes and green with fresh coriander, and a very hot coconut chutney, pale green with the chillies and tart with tamarind, and I tell her it's the best meal I've ever eaten in my whole life and it's a fact. Their little daughter comes and sits next to me while I am eating.

'Sores on your hands?' she asks.

'I'm a bit in the wars,' I answer.

'What's that mean *in the wars*, Mum?' she asks.

'Let him be, lass, let him be,' she says.

'Sorry, a meeting later in the night, no beer,' Vasenn adds, meaning a beer might have helped me forget my wrists, 'Next time, maybe!'

After the meal, Vasenn's wife comes back with cups of coffee steaming on a tray. 'Samarel Coffee, made with caramel,' she says.

The perfume makes me giddy.

*

The night becomes studded, jewels in a crown, with meetings. All around the Medinn sugar estate.

Vasenn and I leave Vikas at the Sebel Social Centre to do one, and Toni does another near his home in Plezans, where there's a tarpaulin put up especially. And we set off for a third in Banbu. It'll start at half past eight at the union offices there.

'It's a home game here,' Vasenn says. And it's true. A huge meeting, where everyone present already knows what's going on. Attention is paid to detailed planning. What to do if '*a*' happens, and what to do if '*b*', as they put it. Contingencies.

'See?' Vasenn says, as we leave. Yes I do.

One last one at Basin, at half past nine, under a tree. Short meeting with lorry drivers. Key sector. They are the ones who carry more than half the labourers to their respective fields. Arrange to meet them at four next morning at the lorry garage.

Vasenn will come himself, he says.

It's a weak point, he says. Where the overseers might put the pressure on them to stay away.

That's how he works, Vasenn.

It's bedtime now.

I'm so tired I could die.

Vasenn stops near the CNT garage, which is where I ask him to drop me. So that I can get my head straight before walking the few blocks home. *Without my errand in my pocket. I see it being catapulted out into the field. Without my bag with my Baya's bangle in it. Left in the dark at a pile of rocks. Without my T-shirt, buried in the sand at Flikanflak. Wearing someone else's pullover. Dog-tired.*

He gets out of the car and comes round to shake my hand. Then he hugs me, and says, 'In just one day. Funny that. But it happens that way sometimes. Like you've joined.

'And,' here he is a bit more serious, 'You're a friend already. All I can say is, well, think about things. We need you, Krish. We like you, Krish. Think about it.'

He hugs me again.

'I've got a question,' I say. I don't even know where it came from. 'Can you think of . . . do you know of anyone who is in any group that, you know, looks after, kinda cares for people condemned to death?'

'What?' He stands there and looks at me in amazement. Maybe even in admiration.

'Well, yes,' he says, 'sure. I can introduce you to someone I know. She's in this group against the death penalty. If you like, I can take you to the first meeting you go to.'

I say we can look at the details tomorrow.

'Or if it can wait, the day after,' he says, putting his head back and laughing. Laughing at me.

And he is off in the old Toyota Corolla.

My whole being is alive.

My head spinning.

I feel a loosening of my arms and legs. I feel my head rise up on my neck. I feel myself relax.

At long last, present and future unify in me. Right at this moment.

Funny, isn't it?

*

I stand and watch Vasenn's car go up the road, and then I try and work out what time of night it can be. I've lost track again.

Maybe it's just after eleven.

Quite late, by my parents' standards. I hesitate to go back home just like that. I mean, what will I say to them?

What should I avoid saying to them? I can't picture what it's like at home any more. It seems so far away. So quiet, such a lost and ignorant place. So echoey and so full of furniture. Such close-by walls in my room. The burglar guards. The things that need throwing away. And the sound of my mother's voice and swishing saris.

And then I feel a distance from her. From her innocent culpability and culpable childishness.

And from the red taxi. From my father's present absence and his absent presence.

I don't feel so strangled by them now. It all seems outside of me now.

And I can breathe.

But, right now. What should I do *now*? Now? Suddenly, there are all sorts of possibilities ahead of me, in my life. My future – the next few minutes of it for a start – lies in my own hands. For just this moment, I feel it. *I can decide.* I decide to think, to think clearly, before just going home. What to tell, what not to tell?

Let me find a place where I can lean against something while I think.

So, that's how I end up going and just leaning against the outside wall around the Compagnie Nationale de Transport building. My back to the wall, one foot up against it, an ad for chocolates painted on the wall behind me, I still remember. I stand in front of the ad. Bar it. Hide it from view. Not that there is anyone to look at it. I look straight ahead and begin to get down to the serious matter of *thinking*. Reflection. Dreaming is my habit already. So, I just need to learn to focus better. Then it might be nearer to thinking. I hear my mother's voice, 'Since nursery school you've been like that.'

As I think of my mother, I start to laugh. *Her errand.* In

the middle of some sugar-cane field. Will someone find it? Appreciate it? Or will all that soggy rain just send it back into the earth? Maybe to sprout next spring.

Maybe I'll have to go and get her another *puliah* from Mamu Dip. Nothing wrong with that. Tell her I lost it. Her lookout. Funny that. I'm not worried any more. It's just a fact now. I, Krish, have lost a *puliah* of marihuana. How can this be remedied? Do I want to remedy it? Why not? Tell her to go get it herself. Weigh the risks. I lift up my two hands in front of my eyes, and look at them. They are my own. I can use them how I want to. They are not tied any more. My eyes are not blindfolded either. I can look where I want to and see what I want to see. This pleases me. My mouth is not gagged. This means I can sing any songs I like. Say what I want to. I can judge things. I can discern people, maybe even my mother and father.

But, now, right now, I've got to decide how much truth and how many lies to tell my mother and father. How much truth is it *right* that I should tell them? How much truth is it my responsibility *not* to tell them?

I am not eighteen yet, so I can't just say that nothing I do is their business, because it so happens that isn't true.

In any case, I live in *their* house.

That, for a start, is their business. Reluctantly, I admit.

But there are some things that I know don't concern them at all. That are none of their business. My thoughts, secret thoughts, for example, are none of their business, even if I'm only seventeen. Even if I was only ten. Not to mention my body. That belongs to me, it's mine.

So, what to tell them? What not to tell them? Not so easy.

A calm spell comes down. A calm spell in my life. '*Wait*

for the moment of the calm spell,' I say to myself, re-membering the words of the salt-pan worker on sick leave who we left the leaflets with. He was a bit drunk, so I hadn't taken note of what he said at the time, but now it comes back to me. Just that. *Wait for the moment of the calm spell. Don't rush at things*, he said, *wait for the moment of the calm spell*. That was how he thought the strike would be a success later in the year.

Right now I must do just that. Wait for the moment of the calm spell. And I've got one coming on right now.

Now.

Just as I'm on the verge of becoming a grown-up. Resolutions resolutions resolutions.

I'll take my life in hand. Make my own decisions. I'll move out of that space between hollow dreams and forced drudgery. I'll move out of that rut, where I never live for the moment itself, but where I'm always trapped between the future of some exam result and the past of my lost friend, my brother, Baya. Who I am parted from for ever. Who I'm no longer part of.

And another thing. I'm also not my mother's little boy any more. Nor someone my father can drive to and from everything.

I am me. No more, no less. Even if my Baya was still here next to me now, I would not be just the little brother of my big brother either.

Quite suddenly I announce to myself, 'You aren't a pathetic shadow of your brother.'

And now it comes to me. A wave of anger. Fury. For the first time, it is pure and harsh anger. Born of that peaceful moment. 'Why did he have to die?' And the rage is out now. There outside of me. As I stand leaning on the wall of the CNT garage, it leaves me, is outside of me. And I can turn towards the wall now, and hit that hard rock wall with a clenched fist. Once, then another time. Hard as hell. Hurt my fist. And a third time.

Then I turn around again. Calming.

I feel the anger subsiding. *Shanti shanti shanti.*

The night is calm and sweet. Raat ke rani perfumes the air. A leaf flies through the air in front of me. Carried by an invisible breeze. A dusty, pale-pink plastic bag murmurs to me from where it is wrapped around a lamppost.

An old van of some kind goes past up the hill. A bicycle freewheels downhill. An ancient car goes up. One or two of the last CNT drivers and conductors are walking to nearby houses, talking in low voices. In open conspiracy.

I overhear words: 'Talk to the men on line fifty-two. Sometimes they a nuisance. Tell them wait a few months, the real thing. Keep in touch with us. And tell them to take those individual bus drivers on line six in hand as well. Cowboys, they are, relatives of the owners. Need to be worked on, with lots of care.'

Yesterday I would not have *heard* these words. And if I, by some chance, had heard them, I wouldn't have understood them. Not at all. They would have been sounds with no meaning. Things that go in one ear and out the other. I was *that* ignorant. And it's only a day later. I'm not so young, nor so ignorant now.

Two nights. Just two nights I've been out. I take a deep breath and pick up the perfume of the raat ke rani again.

'I'm ready now, let me go back home.' I almost say it aloud.

*

As I turn to go, from right behind me I hear the voice of a young girl. Not possible. Imagination.

'Can you help me?' she asks, a voice from the shadows.

'Me?' I ask, 'Me help you?'

'Yes, you.' Wherever did *she* come from? The same breeze that had brought the leaf blew her in? Appeared in the moment of the calm spell? A glimpse of her hair lifting above her ear now. The wind rippling her light shawl. She spoke to *me*? Did the ladybird send her? Strange *déjà vu*. As if I know her already. And I can't even see her yet.

'You won't help me? I think you will. I've been waiting so long. Waiting for someone to approach, for someone I could speak to. I hoped I'd meet another girl or a woman. But no girls, nor any women came past. Only men. And me, in my hour of need.' *In her hour of need*. Strange old-fashioned words.

'What are you asking me to do? I don't know if I can do it.'

'I'll explain. Oh, please say you will help me. Please.' Something familiar about her, the way she moves.

'Explain first.' I can't find words.

'It's simple really. I got permission from my family to come to the discotheque here, up the road, Sam's Disco.'

'Then?' Words are suddenly important to me. She is telling me something, and I am understanding. Ludicrous thought.

She tells me they never let her go out, her mother and her granny. It's the first time they ever agreed. She lives down the Basin Road, near the Kenedi Housing Estate. Supposed to meet up with a group of her school friends near here, just outside the disco. She points up the road. A beautiful arm.

'At eleven we were supposed to meet up. They are all

from Porlwi. Were coming up on the last bus. But the last bus came and went without them. So they aren't coming. Or they came before I got here. I can't go into a disco on my own. Or maybe they've had some problem. I don't know what's happened to them. Last bus gone now. I've never set foot in a disco before, so I'm scared to go and look inside, just in case they aren't in there. Never been out at night before. My mother gave in today because of my results. She let me. But now look what's happened. Say you will help me!'

I explain that I can't see what the problem is, and I can't see what I can do to help her. Her hair lifts in the wind. Winnowing wind.

'I want to go home,' she half stutters. 'But you see, I told my mother and my granny that friends would walk me home. Accompany me. Chaperone me I suppose. This was the condition that she agreed to. *Right to the doorstep*, my mother insisted. That was our arrangement. Now I can't find my friends. I'm scared to go on standing here. I've been hiding in the shadows here. And I'm scared to walk home by myself. And I'm scared to arrive home without some friend to accompany me. She'll never let me go out again in my whole life if I turn up all alone, in the middle of the night. I don't know what to do.'

'So, what you're . . .' I start saying.

'I watched your friend drop you here. I watched the way you spoke. How he hugged you. You were nice to each other. Sort of gentle. Tender even, excuse me saying so. I've never seen men talking to each other like that. I only live with women anyway. And the way he held you like that. Such close friends. You must have known each other for years. You seem a kind boy. I was looking at you. I was watching you. I was even studying you. Then I saw you turn around and hit the wall. Yes, you gave two hard punches against the wall. Then a third. Then a calm. You were so peaceful. A smile came on to your face. I don't know if I can ask you to do this?'

'Ask anyway,' I try to say, but the words don't come out easy.

There is a silence, as she thinks it over. She thinks she has already asked me.

And in that silence, I ask, 'Would you like me to offer to walk you home? Is that what you're asking me to do?'

'Mmm,' she starts to say something, then bows her head, and then decides against bowing her head. She keeps her head up high, and leaves it at that. Yes, that is what she is asking of me.

'Certainly. With pleasure. Of course I'll walk you home. I'm . . .' I start to introduce myself.

But, at the same time, she's started talking, too.

'I'm called Girl. It's only a nickname. Silly, but there it is. I'm called Girl. Girl. Ever heard anything so *stupid*? You can also call me Girl. Everyone else does. What's your name then?'

Car headlights come nearer and light up her face. I see her for the first time. In that moment I realize that it's her. She's the girl I saw walking up the Kandos hill, with the bouncing hair, the poised neck. I saw her touching the posters on the Telecom building. And her name!

I don't know what to say. Should I say I'm Krish? That's what I would normally have said. But, now, of course, I hesitate. What should I say to her?

I am in disarray. My feelings are all muddled. Confused. I feel I'm falling.

'You won't believe this. But at home, at home they call me Boy. It gets on my nerves. I hate it. But there you are.'

She starts to laugh, and then she puts her head back and laughs out loud into the night. A rippling laughter that seems to go on outwards, into the night. Generous. Her laugh makes time stop. A lull. A *lanbeli*.

That name of mine makes her so happy.

'But my friends call me Krish. What you laughing at? Why are you laughing at me?'

'I'll call you whatever you say. I'm just laughing because I'm called Girl. It's silly, isn't it.'

'Rather you call me Krish. But it's up to you.' And then I also start to laugh at our names.

'Yes, ridiculous. Boy and Girl. No one would need names at all if all parents were like ours. But if Girl is good enough for me, I don't see why Boy isn't good enough for you. It's only a name, Krish. I'll wait and see. Time will tell.'

Time.

She wants to see me again? Time will tell.

Krish, I explain, is the name my Baya used to tell everyone to call me. He made them call me Krish. He knew I didn't like being called Boy. But parents don't see anything. They don't realize things. They just go on and on calling me Boy. My proper name is Krishnadev. I don't use it much though. Just on papers. And, as I'm telling her this, I remember the last time I saw it, up on the bulletin board at the school. The fact of failing so far away now. Puny. Petty. I hardly recognize my memory of it. It's so stale.

Girl laughs half to herself. I don't know what at. She's forgotten she's in trouble.

'I've also got a funny name on my papers. I won't tell you what it is. That's why I don't mind being called Girl, frankly. They called me after my grandmother. Name doesn't suit me, I don't think so anyway. Not that it even suits her,' she says. I watch her as she speaks. Sculpted in that light. She smells like heaven. I realize I don't feel any pain any more. Even my wrists have stopped burning. My whole being sings.

She tells me her granny is in the Senior Citizens Club, a leader of their association, and she runs a nursery school, too. Yes, she's still working. You wouldn't believe how many children from Kenedi and Basin have been through her hands. 'That's how she says it: *Been through my hands*.'

Girl's mother is a seamstress. With her tape measure over her shoulder all the time, she says, indicating it with her hand. Her hand is so perfect, and her movements make me see her mother's tape measure.

And with pins in her mouth. She purses her mouth closed and speaks her next words as if she's got pins in her mouth: 'She is her own boss, so she works all the time.' Then her face clouds over, I see it in the light of the street lamp: 'Lots of people she sews for never pay, though. "On Sunday", they say. That's what they say: "On Sunday." Often, when times are hard, when I need things for school, we just sit waiting for people to come and pay on Sunday. Often they don't come ever. I haven't got a father.'

I want to hold her to me.

'Shall we start to walk really slowly,' I ask her. She is deep in thought now. 'Walk slowly, shall we? Don't want your mum and granny upset. We can say the others didn't come, and I've walked you home. You haven't got a father, you said?'

We start to walk close together. Down the hill. It's so easy. So downhill.

'My father left us long ago. I don't understand what happened. Just that in our house there is no father, there are no grandfathers and no brothers either. On my birth certificate there isn't a father either. Never even missed having one. Like that family-planning advertisement. *Aren't there men anywhere around this little island?*

'They think I'm dancing away, my mum and gran. Until two in the morning. What time are you expected home? Some particular time?'

'No,' I say it with a certain pride, as though my parents never had that sort of control over me. Never.

As though I am a free man. Not a servant you can call 'Garson!' Not a child. Not a stunted little boy.

'They think I'll be back from the Uncle Dip's place at the very earliest tomorrow morning. My mother sent me on an errand. To pick up something there. I'd just got my results, *fail* by the way, I take it you passed, congratulations! Anyway the old lady said I should go and see Mamu Dip and Renuka Mami. She noticed how down I was, that's what I think. For once, she respected my feelings. I was supposed to stay there two or three, or maybe even three or four days. I'm not expected back today. Either tomorrow or the next day.'

When I say this, there is a deep silence.

We are both scared. I realize we are free for at least three hours. *Déjà vu.* She also realizes it no doubt. Fear of freedom makes me giddy.

I who have never walked around at night with a young girl. I who have never walked around with a young girl even in the day. And she's never been to a discotheque. Never been out at night.

'Boy and Girl,' I think to myself, and there's a laugh inside me.

'That friend of yours who dropped you, who is he? The one who drove you up to the CNT garage? Was that your Uncle Dip?'

'No. Not at all.' And here, at this moment, I take a firm resolution. I will not tell her any string of lies. However complicated it is, however unbelievable, I'll tell her the truth.

'But where had you come from? What were you two doing? Who is that who dropped you? Where does your Uncle Dip think you are?'

'What can I say? It's a long story. Let's walk on. Rather you tell me about yourself. I promise I'm not hiding anything, and I won't hide anything. It's just a bit complicated. And long.'

So, she tells how she was at Maurice Curé High School and she's also just got her results, and she *has* passed. And she was going to be meeting friends from Maurice Curé at the discotheque. She wants to leave school now, but her mother thinks she should go back and repeat the year to try and improve her results. Girl wants to go out to work instead. *Get out there and get a job*, as she puts it. An *employer*, I think to myself, and laugh. Her mother being a seamstress, and with a family renting a few rooms from them, life is not easy. Not enough income to keep up with the maintenance of the place. Perhaps she will get a place for nursing, she says.

She's like that, all decided and calm. She'll be good at that I should think, looking after sick people. She looks strong enough. I walk slowly next to her.

And then she can earn something while she's studying nursing, she says. Become a skilled worker. That's what she wants. Then her family can get by better.

'You talk so differently about things,' I say. 'Your ideas are all in order in your head. And I like your voice, too. Modulated. You move about, like . . . like my Aunt Renuka.'

And as I say this, I realize I'm falling, falling for Girl. Falling in love with Girl.

It's quite sudden, and like actually falling. From a high place.

This no one had ever told me.

So I say, 'I like the way you and your mother and granny live together like that. A warm kind of family. I like that.' Inside of me, I could die.

'As for me,' she says, 'I still like the way you got out of that car, and your friend came and hugged you, and the way you walked over to that wall. You were so deep in thought. You would never have noticed me. You seemed so engrossed, making up your mind about something so important. And yet you look so young. And hitting the wall like that.'

'I think doing nursing sounds a good thing,' I say, veering off the subject of me, because it invites lies. 'You should stand up to your mother on this. It's a good point. I'm not always like that. I used to do everything my mother and father told me to, no matter how wrong it was for me to do it. I don't know why I was like that. Have you applied already? For nursing, I mean?'

'Yes. I'll hear soon. Then I'll know. I just have to inform them about my HSC results. I should be accepted, because they take young people with SC as well. When you were speaking you said you *used to* do everything your parents told you to. Why *used to*? You don't any more?'

'So many things have happened to me since I left Renuka Mami's house and got on to the bus home, I can't quite get used to it. A sort of misunderstanding. A sort of shift in my destiny. A sort of cowardice because I get seasick. The day before yesterday was it? Yes, the day before yesterday. Since then, so many things have happened to me. My parents don't know anything about it all. That's why I was standing there, thinking. I was trying to work out what to tell them and what *not* to tell them. How much truth and how many lies? And what a son should or should not tell parents. What is not their rightful concern at all.'

'And why punch the wall?'

'That was something else. That, that was because of something sad. A loss. The death of my big Baya. He died so young. It was two years ago, it was, but I never felt it. And over the past two days, I've *been through* his death. So, I don't feel like it was my fault he died any more. I don't resent so much that he was better than me at everything. These last two days I let my sorrow in, and then it's gone out again. What you think it was? Delayed-reaction mourning? You know, before now, his death had been smothering me. Exams had added to it all, making me put off my pain till another day. And making me feel all cramped inside. Even stunted. He died two whole years ago, and then it was only these past two days that I *felt* it. I nearly cried,' then I correct that, 'I *did* cry actually. I cried my eyes out. Not once. Twice. And then a third time. And then, after the sorrow was out, I felt cross at his death. A fierce anger in me. So I hit the wall like that. Does it sound stupid? I'm not even sure I understand it myself. But it is the nearest to the truth I can get.'

'That's very sad. Him dying,' she says, 'And you obviously loved him so much. Your brother.'

And so it struck me that we were *two* different people. Baya and I were *separate*. I'd always been too close, so close I was part of him. As if we were a pair of twins. And the idea that I *loved* him makes me see him separate from me.

Girl wouldn't have confused him and me. Nor would she necessarily have preferred him to me. She says she likes *me*. Likes the way I talk, the way I walk, the way I hit that wall when I thought nobody was looking. She likes the way I had to take a decision all by myself. She likes the way I loved my Baya.

And me. What do I think? What do I feel?

I feel I'm falling.

Not for this or that reason really.

Just falling.

Just because of the way she came up and spoke to me? The way her mind works? But even before that, I had started to love her. From when the light from the street lamp reflected in her hair. The way her hair moved. Silly, but true. Her hair moving like that. Like a dance. The way she moves her body when she talks, like a tree she is. She changes position slowly, exactly like a big tree in the trade winds. Her husky voice. The way she works things out. Her questions. All of that. And all this doesn't go halfway to *explaining*. It doesn't explain why I feel what I feel as we are walking down this road this night. And even before that, from when our paths crossed on the day I set off.

'Emotions haven't got explanations, have they? Otherwise they wouldn't be emotions. Or if they did have explanations, they might be infinitely long.' I say all this to her. Things I never even thought before. Never even knew I could think about.

Then I take her hand in mine. Electricity. *Coup de foudre.*

Happiness, joy, contentment, excitement. All in one scramble inside me. Through my own hand. My ordinary hand. The same hand that just swings next to me when I walk about. The hand that itched to snuff out my life.

And I am not the I that I was before.

I have changed. Now I'm calm. Now I act in a rhythm of my own. I'm someone new. And yet still the same old boy.

Her hand is cool in my hand; she's been out in the cold longer than I have.

We stop walking, and I look at her. Just like in my dream, I lift the hair from the side of her neck, but this time I say: 'Do you think I could kiss you, just here, on your neck?'

'Yes,' she says, that's all she says, 'Yes.'

Which is what I do.

Then I ask her if it isn't ridiculous, I've only just met her and I am kissing the corner of her neck like this?

'Yes, it is,' she says, 'ridiculous. Especially in Payot, of all places. Where all the broken-down buses are.'

So we walk on in silence. I don't know what will happen next. Anything can be waiting for me just down the road. The future is waiting for me. The future is in my own hands, or our own hands. Here, just ahead of us. Step by step, as we make headway.

For two days now, I haven't known what will happen next, and it isn't stopping now.

She stops. I do too. She puts her arms around me and I hold her close. She moves even closer.

'My turn now,' she says. 'Can I kiss you just there. On your ear lobe?'

I could die now, I think. When she kisses my ear, my legs go weak.

'I think I'm falling, falling in love,' I whisper.

'Mutual,' she says.

'But I'm going to walk you home now, and leave you at home really fast,' I announce, to my own surprise. 'I'm not used to this kind of feeling.'

'Yes, you'd better do just that,' she says.

And we begin to run between the street lamps, and slow down under them. To look into one another's eyes.

But the only thing is, I know it and I think she knows it too, it would be quite possible for us to make love right now. Which is partly why we run away from it.

I stop, and pull her to a halt.

I'll take her home. And sing all the way back home. Tiredness has lifted off me.

I ask her to meet me at the Banbu court the next morning. Before she goes and finds out about nursing college. I'll have to go to the court, I explain. I am a day late.

What does that mean? Will I be arrested on the spot? Humiliated? What will she think?

One thing I know is that I can't hide this from her.

She doesn't even ask me why I suggest so strange a rendezvous.

She just laughs.

'Yes,' she says.

✳

As I walk home, it is as though my feet aren't touching the ground. And my head still sings with her perfume.

I reach the bit of street in front of my parents' house in Karo Lalyann. I stand there. It isn't town and it isn't countryside. It isn't paradise and it isn't hell. It's a place of boredom. Where people wait for better times. Maybe for ever. The loneliness of the town and the rut of the country.

All this goes through my head as I stand in front of their gate. Hedge on both sides. Red-leaf hedge, shining maroon in the streetlight. I put my hand out to a leaf and run my fingers over it. I know this leaf so well, and it knows me so well. My mother's tulsi tree in front of the window. The pinkness of the house. I was the one who did the actual painting of it. For the New Year. Look, there are the signs of my bad workmanship. Drops of pink paint on the windowpanes.

The house lies there, quiet. Not even the television on. Of course, it's too late. They leave one or two lights on. In case of burglars. Not that there's much to steal. One television set. A video player. A rice cooker. A refrigerator, if they'd steal that. My computer. But it's like they are locked up inside. Prisoners.

Again the perfume of raat ke rani wraps around me. From the neighbours' garden? It must be the season. Could drug me.

Silence. A lone toad croaks. From the market gardener's dam nearby. Another toad replies now. Then more, until there is a cacophony.

My father's taxi isn't back from Goolam Panelbeaters yet. Peace be on its absence.

But then again, it's not that I *have* to go in my father's car. I could kick myself. As though I was ever forced to go in it.

I just say no, that's all. Simple.

Not everything is open to choice. But that is one of the things that is. Even my father has rebelled. He doesn't believe in the gods. And he says so. No one can force even *him* to believe in god. And if I hadn't bothered to ask, I would never have known. He who seems so submissive, so resigned. But isn't.

My parents' house looks nicer to me now. From this point of view. From the outside. Some magnetism inside the house that's pulling me in towards it. Coconut-cake pink and all. With burglar guards. In concrete. Now that I am outside of it, free to go in or come out, free to stand and look at it. Now that it's something *outside* me like that, separate from me, I can like it. I'm coming home. But not to *my* home. To my parents' home. The return of the prodigal. *Lakaz mama*. To where I am at home. Home. *Om. Shanti*. For the first time, I think of home as a place of potential rest.

A place from which I can regenerate myself for another tomorrow. So that I don't have to sleep under the shadow of piles of rocks, nor in abandoned sheds. I don't have to stand leaning against walls all night. I can come back here. And why? Because it isn't my house any more. It is my parents' house. *Lakaz mama*. That's what it is. And I have left it. Left it behind me. I've got a new home somewhere in the future ahead of me. *Om shanti shanti shanti*.

Between two lives, a moment of calm. Watch out for it. It's here. Right here.

And so it is that I take another resolution. I will go out and find a place of my own. A room of my own. Soon as I turn eighteen. Soon as I can afford it. Work. I'll have to look for a boss too. Vasenn and Vikas are right. *A fact*. Always keep track of a bad fact. Otherwise you haven't got much hope of changing it.

A rented room, or a bit of leased land that I can build a tiny house on. Just one room. Or take up a bit of land illegally somewhere, people do it. So that I can maybe think about the future, not just the one day ahead of me. Not just for me, but for other people. With other people. They are all around me.

A place from where maybe, just maybe, I, like a stream, can bubble forth from my own source. Me, Boy. Me, Krish.

I, who can be part of the pleasures of life, the dangers of life, the love of life, and maybe even the commitment to life. Me, Boy. Me, Krish.

My parents are free now. They will like that. They are free of me. I'm off their hands now.

Look how they live happily without me. I think of them getting up, going about their daily lives, just the same when I'm not there.

They are at ease because I am at Mamu Dip and Renuka Mami's house in Montayn Long. They think of me all settled there, sleeping away. In one place. Relaxed and safe. Enjoying the company of Mamu Dip, getting over my exam results. Him making me forget I failed. Maybe they are healing from the loss of their first-born son, only now. At long last. Who knows? That's their secret. Maybe they will just accept me however I turn out. Maybe they will have to.

They have got themselves used to the idea that I will repeat. They think I will do another year at school. But I don't think I will. I'll give myself these next days to think about that. Plenty of time. Then I'll take my decision. There are so many other things to do. What's the point in repeating?

'Goodnight,' I said to Girl, 'Goodnight.' Just that. I didn't need to say *I love you* or anything like that. Not just then, because she already knew. Whenever she's in doubt, I'll tell her. And I knew then she loved me. Just then, at least. And I am flooded with the memory of how she moves her body when she talks. A tree. And my whole body goes warm with the memory. And her hair. Just by her neck. And her body is still imprinted on mine. Memory is in my body, not just in my mind. I can smell her on me.

I'll see her tomorrow. Girl.

'Bye,' I said to Vasenn, earlier.

'Good luck,' he said to me, as he hugged me to him. 'Keep in touch. Come meet us at Basin for the meeting with the drivers, where they start up the tractors. At the very bottom of Basin Street. At four in the morning. We'll be there till five. We'll wait until quarter past five in case you turn up. I will, anyway, in person.'

'I want to know what happens next.'

'Yes, try it and see!' And off he drove into the night. Gone.

I'll see him tomorrow. Vasenn.

And there's Captain and Kid. Probably did get their bail this morning. Them and Jon-Jon. Will they come by and visit me one day? It seems ages since we were in that limousine together. Only the day before yesterday. Will Captain have moved house? Will Kid's wife have kicked him out because of drink? Will Major and Chanchal move house along with Captain?

And then it dawns on me once again. The thought is always escaping, and then rushing back. What will happen? I was supposed to turn up at the Banbu court *yesterday*. I have stood my own lawyer up. I didn't appear before the magistrate. Will there be an arrest warrant out for me? Will I have to telephone James Bronson in the morning? Lucky I remember his name. I'll have to borrow money to pay him. I touch my pocket. The stash the robber gave me. It makes me laugh. Illgotten gains. And I'll go to the court today. She'll be there. Girl. Maybe I'll have to stand in the box and apologize to the magistrate for not turning up or something. Maybe say I was hurt, show my wrists. Be asked to get a medical certificate. Who knows? And about the dead girl, will they still be blaming Captain and the Kid and me?

It's past one o'clock in the morning.

All signs of tiredness are gone. I forget the court.

I feel quiet and at peace. I sit on the step in front of our house now. And I think. For three days I haven't been stuck in that rut, thinking interminably about myself and my exams and nothing else. There's a whole world out there. To be in. I've stepped out of my cocoon world. I've been prised out. By events. Like a snail from its shell. I've started to fend for myself. I've fallen in love. With someone called Girl, if you can believe such a thing.

I feel her goodnight kiss. Her lips still on mine. My body is alive with hers. Her smell is on my body, in my clothes.

I've been linked to events, part of them. Maybe I'll be in a strike in a few months' time. I've already participated in preventing a false strike. Soon I may go to another meeting, this time with lorry drivers. I *feel* my memories of being with Vasenn, Vikas, and Toni. Will they be friends? I like them. And they say they like me.

And even that band of robbers who found me by the pile of rocks in the cane fields, they didn't kill me. They just left me somewhere. Not because they like me, though. Because dead bodies are bad luck. I shake my head. The people I've met. Why did I think I'd never meet people like that?

And the warmth of eating peanuts at sunset with Captain and Kid. Loving the taste of life. Every second of it. They feel it as it passes. I want to be like them. I will go to the Banbu police station on the way to the court in the morning, just in case they haven't got bail yet. Not that I would know what to do if they haven't. But *people* look after these things. And I'm a person. Otherwise, I'll go see

183

them at Pwentosab. On the weekend, maybe. Or tomorrow, after the meeting with lorry drivers. After the court.
I'll just go down to the fish-landing station and wait for
them. Ask around. I want to see them again. I feel a need to
see them again.

And, as I sit here, I am saying goodbye to the mermaid.
For she is dead. And in memory of her, I will go visit the
girl from India in prison. She is alive. Is that a kind of thing
a person can do? Why not? I think to myself. Maybe she
hasn't got any visitors at all. And Vasenn will take me
to a meeting against the death penalty. He said so. To a
meeting with other people. Likeminded.

Not only all that.

I've said goodbye now, at last, at long last to my Baya
too. I bend down and touch my shoes, *his* running shoes
are my shoes now.

I say goodbye to him. To him, too.

Ah, his bracelet, the bangle with his name engraved on it.
I'll have to go and look for it, next to the pile of rocks.
Tomorrow. A memento. Maybe I will wear it. Now that I've
cried for him. The pain lessens. It's going. Only some of the
anger stays on. This is normal. Everything to its time.

Not only that.

Then, I realize it, I am launching myself like this on a
speech, preparing the conversation, choosing these difficult words one by one, struggling for phrases sacred
enough to say goodbye to my old self.

I sing the words: *Easy come, easy go*.

I get up and stand facing the front door. I knock on it.
As a young man should. Coming to visit two older people
who he is fond of.

'Who's there?' My father always asks. Slightly scared
tack in his voice. His way, that. It used to irritate me, but it

doesn't any more. He is *like* that. Taxi drivers worry about hold-ups, about being hijacked, about their money being stolen. He is just like that.

'Who's there?'

I stand there thinking. What should I answer? What should I call myself? And suddenly I know.

'Boy,' I call out, 'It's Boy.'

What does it matter if they call me Boy at home? What could it matter? I'm growing up anyway. I'll be eighteen anyway. What's in a name anyway? Anyway. Anyway. Anyway.

I pick up the front-door key from under the doormat. Any robber could find it. Under the doormat. I shake my head and laugh. *So classical*, I think to myself. And this thought is important: That I can judge them this way. Call them *classical*.

I open the door and go in quietly.

'Is this a time for a son to saunter in singing?' my mother screeches. Her sibilants don't get on my nerves any more. They are funny. And she heard me singing.

'Not really,' I reply. 'It *is* a bit inconsiderate, I agree. Not a time to come knocking on the door, you're right on that one, Ma. But no need to worry, I'm OK. Everything's OK.'

I go past my granddad and granny's wedding photograph still hanging high up on the wall, straight through to the pantry. And there I find a bowl of lentil soup with bringals in it, and a couple of bits of dried snoek fish fried crisp, a tiny bowl of hot tomato chutney, no more than a spoonful and a bowl of white rice. She knew I was coming? I pour some tea from the thermos on the table. Left there for me? I sit down and enjoy my food. Spoilt brat. She left all this just in case? Even if she was sure I wouldn't be home, she left some in case?

There is even a portion of maize pudding. I take it out, put it on a small plate and eat it too.

I walk through the house to my cocoon room. As I'm walking through my door, cream-coloured paint still peeling off it, I take a decision. *I will set my alarm clock for just before four*. I'll definitely go and meet Vasenn. The thought makes me happy, just that *thought*. Maybe I'll find out about the movement he's in. I'll find out from the inside, by being in it. Then I can see what happens.

I undress, and sit down naked at my desk. For real. This time, one foot is up on the chair next to me. I lean back and check my wrists. Better my mother doesn't see these cuts. I'll have to get out a long-sleeved shirt to cover them. But from now on, I'm going *out*. Into the world. Breech or not.

I won't stay behind the burglar guards any more. Prisoner by my own choice, oh no.

Everything that has started will continue.

I will be *in* it. If there is a little bit I can do, I'll do it. If I don't manage, at least I'll have tried.

Yes, that's what I'll do.

I pick up the blade and almost laugh at myself. I slowly wrap it back into its thin sheath of paper. *Paper covers blade*. Then I open the desk drawer and undo the turquoise snake. And as I straighten the rope out, and coil it into a loose spiral, I feel some huge knot in me gets undone. First loosened and then undone. Not tied up in circles any more.

I take the seethrough plastic bag of white powder, too white and crystalline, and I seal it into an envelope. I'll give it to the market gardener later. He can make use of it. Or maybe he doesn't agree with using it. I'll ask him.

I go over to my bed, take the oil bottle full of kerosene from under it and put it by the door. It's on its way out now.

'Boy?' My mother's voice. 'Everything OK, Boy? You brought me my stuff, Boy?' It's my mother, just asking this as small talk, I can hear. Her and her *puliah* of gandya. Me and my cannabis trip. What am I going to tell her?

I notice consternation in her voice. Not just nagging. But some real fear.

'Thanks for the food you left out for me, Ma. You spoil me! We'll talk about everything in the morning, or in the afternoon, maybe,' I say. 'I'll be going out very early in the morning. Don't worry if you find I've gone out. I'll be back around midday. Or a bit later. Then we can talk. OK?'

'It's a pleasure, Boy. But how did you get here at this time of night? Walking or what? And the mission? You haven't answered me. The errand? Is everything OK?'

I don't need to answer. Rhetorical question.

I haven't got her errand. We'll sort that out. Maybe I'll have to go to Mamu Dip's again.

But somehow I'm free.

I set the alarm for four and stand the clock next to the bed.

I lie there in bed, thinking for what seems like ages. With the bedside light on. Then I hear the quiet tiptoeing of my mother. And a knock at my door.

'Yes?' I say.

She comes in and closes the door behind her, puts a finger to her lips to say be quiet. My dad mustn't hear this.

'They found you out? Policemen? I've got you into trouble? The errand? It's all my fault!' She sits at the foot of my bed, consternation in her every movement. 'A man telephoned this afternoon. Police officer, he said. Wanted to know where you were. I said at your Mamu Dip's, in Krevker. He said you were supposed to come to some court today. *Very important. Lucky not a warrant. Under age*. Said what kind of a mother am I. They found you out, Boy? Oh, Krish.'

The only thing I hear is her saying my name. Krish. It sounds like music from her lips. To my ears.

So I smile.

She relaxes when she sees me smile.

'Don't worry about a thing, Mum.' That's all I can say. But my mind is working overtime. I hide my wrists.

'You managed to throw it away before they got it? Before the police even saw it? My errand? The policeman said you have to come to get charges lifted. I didn't know what to say. I was struck dumb.' She obviously hasn't told my father a thing. She hasn't sent word to my Mamu Dip either. She has been panicking all by herself for hours now.

She seems to notice I'm not too worried. And she is always such a hopeful person. She seems so distant from me now. And full of faults and quirks and shortcomings.

So I just say, 'Yes, that's right.'

'But the court,' she insists, 'the policeman. What is it all about?' She wants to know.

'I just have to go to the court because I'm a witness. A witness. I found a body.' She shudders, and then sighs. She is out of her depth now. She is overwhelmed. The world has rushed into her house.

The first thing she wants to know is if I was with her brother at the time.

'Is he in trouble, too?'

I say quite simply, 'No.'

Inexplicably this seems to relieve her. Maybe because only one of her relatives is involved, me.

I know she's got to accompany me to the court. The magistrate will insist. I'm a minor. So I ask her. Could she meet me at the court in Banbu at nine o'clock? Will she tell

188

my father please? That I'm a witness. I've set my alarm, I tell her, because I'm going to a meeting before going to the court.

'A meeting?' she says, as though I have gone completely mad. Or as though she is now beginning to hear things.

'Yes.' That's all I say. 'See you at the court.'

'Krish,' she whispers. 'I was so scared. It would have been my fault. Is it going to be OK?'

'Yes, it'll all turn out fine. Maybe you should join the movement for decriminalizing gandya, Ma? Ha! Ha!'

Again, that's all I say.

'What?' she says. 'You know I'm against drugs.'

'Oh, Ma, you're impossible. Let's talk another day.'

'Sleep well, Krish.'

*

Between the alarm ringing and me getting washed and dressed, there is no time at all. My body both aches and sings. Aches with having been tied up and sings with the wild scope of new love. Feelings, feeling, feelings.

I catch the first bus. Again I overhear a conversation that enthrals me. This time between conductor and driver. *Prepare for the strike in the cane-cutting season.* I find myself thanking the stars and the moon, thanking the air and the sun that hasn't yet risen, thanking every living creature in the universe that I *hear* this conversation, and that when I *hear* it, I know what it means.

I get off at Basin. In that misty darkness. When Vasenn sees me, he goes on talking to the gathered drivers sitting on rocks under trees, maybe thirty of them, and comes and hugs me, and says 'my brother', thus introducing me. Then he goes on drawing their ideas together. As I listen, I begin to realize the meaning of what Vasenn had said the night before. These drivers who pick up the waiting labourers are the key to ruining this false strike. They can carry the message almost everywhere on this estate. They mustn't make any mistake.

Questions are posed. Mulled over.

Jokes get cracked.

More issues discussed.

Again I'm struck by a sort of love amongst these men in this darkness.

The sun is still sleeping.

Then they all begin to move, and I hear ignition keys turning engines in all the lorries and in all the tractors with their trailers with seats on them. Like the immense roar of a lion. Showing everyone who it is that works.

They put on their pairs of lights and set off, filing past us, past Vasenn and me, and they each flick their lights at us. Winking.

Vasenn and I go to Lalwiz and drink a cup of tea at a workers' café bustling with men. Then we set off for a half past six meeting at the Baitka in Banbu. As we go past Montan Bol, I remember my bag, lying somewhere next to the pile of rocks. I've got to get it back.

'Vasenn,' I begin to ask, 'Can we just go two minutes in on the Kaskavel Road? I lost my bag there, and it could get me into trouble.'

'You bloody get me into trouble!' That hard streak again. It scares me. But I understand. For him it is a risk to go into a cane field.

But he turns his car in, and says: 'Hurry up then! Where? Show me where I must drive, for god's sake.'

I recognize what must be my huge pile of rocks, and point it out to Vasenn. He pulls up for me to get out. He will drive to a place where he can turn around, further along the dust track.

I work out where I must have been lying down, where the musk-rat bit me, where the robbers shared their booty. I go and look for my blue denim bag there.

Sure enough.

I pick it up and hug it. I do a quick sega dance with it in my arms. I send my hand down deep inside for my Baya's bracelet. There it is. Safe.

Over my shoulder my bag goes again.

Vasenn is back again, and we are off to the Baitka in Banbu.

Where all the labourers who ride to work by bicycle are passing by to confirm they are all going to work, and where the factory workers are clocking in to say they will be in the mill by seven o'clock as usual.

Again this feeling of warmth and closeness.

By half past seven all is quiet in the Baitka. Some labourers' wives are checking on the news with us.

Then we go and buy bread rolls hot from the bakery on the Royal Road. And that is how we find ourselves sitting down under the enormous badamye trees in the alley leading to the court house. Vasenn says he's got a few hours free now, before meeting up with all the others in Porlwi to see whether the false strike has been successfully broken. So we can talk. I tell him about having to be right here in an hour's time, in the Banbu court. About finding the girl's body when we were out fishing. And I tell him about my dread of the young girl in the newspaper being hanged.

He gets out his mobile phone and rings a number.

'Vasenn here. Remember you invited me to a meeting?'

He listens now.

'Yes, exactly. Yes, I'm fine. Next one, when?'

I watch the rounded contours of this man's face, so expressive.

'I'm bringing someone along, a young man. He's called Krish. Krish Burton.'

He tells me the date, 8 March. To coincide with International Women's Day, he says.

Everything is so easy for him.

Then he says he'll stay with me and come along to see the magistrate. Just in case.

*

As Vasenn and I slowly walk towards the court house, deep in conversation about the real strike next month, stepping over the roots of huge white-barked trees and moving into the dark thick intimate shade of even bigger badamye trees, he hands me the name and telephone number of the girl he has just spoken to in the group against the death penalty. He says he'll come with me to the first meeting, but he makes sure I've also got all the details. That's his way of working.

Then I catch sight of someone running to catch up with us, she's in a yellow and red dress, like flames, flames darting in the sunshine towards me, her arms wide open now, her hair swinging next to her neck. It's Girl.

And I catch her as she leaps into the shade, and into my arms, and I swing her around in the air. I put her down and introduce her to Vasenn.

'She's applied to nursing school,' I say, as an ordinary atmosphere of warmth builds around us. 'Vasenn is in the mill workers' union, a friend of mine,' I say. 'The one that hugged me last night at the bus garage.'

Vasenn, feet on the ground, standing on one of the big roots of one of those huge trees, still worries about the court case against me, not sure charges will have been lifted. 'You never know,' he says, and I'm sure he's right.

He says he didn't know I had a girl. To which I say, 'I didn't either.' And Girl just laughs. My body goes mad with desire again. This dress is also tight around her hips and then swings outwards. Red and yellow. Yellow and red. I remind myself that I'm going to court soon. Going to see a magistrate. That I'm in trouble. I look up at the trees.

And then, coming along the side of the stone wall that borders the dispensary just opposite where we are forming this quiet group, I see some green and pink colours and the way they swish, and I know that they can only be the colours and movement of the sari that is my mother's. There she is. Here she comes. Floating along. Long black hair tied in a loose plait down her back. Casting the end of her sari over her shoulder. Sailing, again, like a ship. I expect to feel anger, but I don't. I just see her like she is. Funny, almost. Muddled and silly.

She is on her own. She hasn't told my father yet, I bet.

I go up to her, and bring her to meet Vasenn and Girl. 'You told Dad?' I ask. She lowers her eyes, meaning no, and says she couldn't because supposedly he had to go and check on his car at Goolam Panelbeaters anyway.

Vasenn leans over and says quietly that, strictly speaking, it's my job to tell my dad anyway. He just interrupts and says it. I note him looking at my mother, almost shaking his head in wonderment, no doubt thinking she is the one who had got me to carry the *puliah* of gandya like that. He is the only one here who knows how close I was to being locked up on extra charges. I realize that, for my mother, it never really sank in. She's forgotten her panic already. Everything is back, floating along in the immensity of the *grande fleuve* of the movement of time. Morality and immorality. Mortality and immortality all mixed up. She'll no doubt think nothing of sending me back to Mamu Dip to get another *puliah* of gandya, to replace the lost one. This time, *I'll* decide though. I won't just pretend I'm a courier.

She is not daunted by the proximity of the court house either. Nor by the hugeness of the trees. She looks Vasenn up and down first, and then Girl, with a mixture of interest, admiration and undisguised suspicion. Wondering if either of them or both of them will have me eating all sorts of things, mainly sausages, the minute she turns her back. Or if they will be getting me into some other trouble. I who am already deep in trouble. They who are here to help me get out of it. My mother once again oblivious to the fact that she was the one who nearly got me into real trouble.

Girl looks rightly pained at being studied in this way. Almost turns away.

Vasenn will, I can feel it, just check we know what we are doing here at the court, and then leave us for his next meeting.

And it is at this strained moment that I hear a vaguely familiar sound. Pleasure. Something almost divine. Something so happy I want to laugh, or even cry. I can't quite work out what it is. And then.

I can't believe it.

It must be my mind making it all up.

It is the sound, the unmistakable sound of the spluttering limousine, screeching to a halt, its engine cutting out, and there it is, in all its maroon glory, standing right next to us. Silent. Peace settling around it.

Both doors fly open and then shut again as Captain and Kid rise up – one huge-framed and the other taut and compact – out of the Mini Traveller, and rush forward to hug me and hold me, laughing and throwing their heads back.

'We were expecting you!' says Captain. As though I was the one who had just walked in.

Then they stand quite still and wait for introductions.

My mother now moves closer to Vasenn and Girl, two distinctly reassuring people by comparison, as the two loud-talking life-loving characters take over the whole stage, now leading me to the magistrate's chambers as if they were my advocate and attorney.

'They arrested two other guys,' Captain says, 'so prosecution's got some other thesis about the murder.'

'Murder,' I hear my mother mumble, grumble.

'Just the right time to get to her,' Captain goes on, 'magistrates are very fussy about time.'

Captain has just abandoned the limousine, parked any old which way, but nevertheless in the right direction for pushing if need be. As if the place were his. He then ushers me, my mother, Girl, Kid and Vasenn along, right up to the clerk's office. Like one of those sheepdogs with their goats.

'This young man has an appointment with the magistrate right now,' announces Captain to the clerk, looking at his watch. 'His mother will accompany him.'

The magistrate looks up at me, my denim bag over my shoulder, and at my mother in all her green and pink.

Panic strikes me, as I realize how little I know my mother. What if she goes and says something about the *puliah* of *gandya*?

But she doesn't. Of course not. She's wily. The magistrate just asks her to sign a piece of paper. *Paper covers blade. Blade cuts rope. Rope ties up paper.*

'Charges against Krish Burton withdrawn,' she sighs, the magistrate does, as if we were wasting her time on purpose, 'It was only a routine arrest,' she says. She hates us.

'Oh,' my mother says, glaring at her, 'is that so now.'

My mother seems to have grown up. In just those few minutes in there, under the power of the magistrate.

'Good day, then!' And out she struts, sternly. Her sari is swishing with a new dignity. I can literally see her mind working things out now. She can smell a happy ending, she can.

Vasenn suddenly pulls me close to my mother and whispers to me: 'Go on, get her to join the movement for decriminalization, Krish!' My mother's heard this before. She glares at him, like she's shocked, and then she laughs.

And then suddenly she looks at me, right at me. And she sees me. 'Yes, we must talk, Krish. We must talk.'

I can't believe my ears. The fact that the words are said. By him. By her. In my presence. As I breathe in, taking the world inside me and feeling it spread out into my arms and hands, into my legs and feet. Into my scalp and then deep into my head. My chest swells. My shoulders take on a firmness. I stand up high now. I feel my voice comes out strong when I talk. I join the people who laugh loud, who stride, who dare to hope.

And so, we make a motley, celebratory group as we

begin to say our goodbyes. Each one going a different way for now, except, of course, for the inseparable Captain and Kid, who will be together.

'Oh, one last thing first,' says Captain, 'A little surprise for you before you go off again.'

He and Kid draw me away from the others, each take an arm, and walk me back to the limousine. It's a special treat for me, Kid tells me. To give me confidence, Captain adds.

I can't imagine what it is.

They point to the window at the rear section of the limousine, where the dogs used to sit behind us.

There they are! Of course. Both of them, Major and Chanchal, wagging their huge white tails as I get nearer to them.

So I put my hand in through the eternally-open front window, and they jump over into the back seat, and start to lick it all over.

'No eating holes in my T-shirts any more,' I warn. 'I'm a man now, so watch out!'

Then I stick my head and shoulders in through the window, and they lick me all over, until my ears can't bear the tickling any more.

When Captain and Kid get in, Captain, with conviction, turns the ignition key. No way. Nothing happens.

So that is how, when Kid gets out and he and I start pushing, Vasenn comes along to help push, too. And how Girl, her red and yellow dress still hugging her hips and then swirling, comes in between me and Kid, and helps to push, touching my chest with her shoulder. And how my scatty mother comes up on the outside of Vasenn, tucks in the end of her green and pink sari, and she, too, pushes on that old maroon-coloured limousine.

The two dogs' white fluffy tails wag against the back windows, a pair of windscreen wipers.

'You see,' Vasenn laughs, 'what a bit of cooperation can do?'

And words coming before the idea even forms in my head, I add: 'And make sure you guys go in the right direction, will you?'

'Well said!' says Vasenn.

In the thick shade of the badamye trees.

I look down at my Baya's running shoes.

I, who don't yet know my own direction. Or do I?

A NOTE ON THE AUTHOR

Lindsey Collen was born in South Africa and
lives in Mauritius. She is the acclaimed author
of *There is a Tide, The Rape of Sita,
Getting Rid of It and Mutiny. The Rape of Sita*
was awarded the 1994 Commonwealth Writers'
Prize. *Boy* is a reworking of her 1996 novel in
Mauritian, *Misyon Garson*.

A NOTE ON THE TYPE

The text of this book is set in Linotype Sabon,
named after the type founder, Jacques Sabon. It was
designed by Jan Tschichold and jointly developed
by Linotype, Monotype and Stempel, in response to
a need for a typeface to be available in identical form
for mechanical hot metal composition and hand
composition using foundry type.

Tschichold based his design for Sabon roman on
a fount engraved by Garamond, and Sabon italic
on a fount by Granjon. It was first used in 1966
and has proved an enduring modern classic.